~~~~~~

A TIME FOR TIGERS

By Robert F. Burgess

A TIME FOR TIGERS

THE MYSTERY OF MOUND KEY

A TIME
FOR TIGERS

Robert F. Burgess

Illustrated by Vic Donahue

THE WORLD PUBLISHING COMPANY

CLEVELAND AND NEW YORK

Published by The World Publishing Company
2231 West 110th Street, Cleveland, Ohio 44102
Published simultaneously in Canada by
Nelson, Foster & Scott Ltd.
Library of Congress catalog card number: 68–14686
Text copyright © 1968 Robert F. Burgess
Illustrations copyright © 1968 Vic Donahue
WP
Designed by Jack Jaget

This book is dedicated to all fishermen,
young and old alike, who know,
or who would like to know,
the thrill of sport fishing for big sharks. And it is
with particular gratitude that I dedicate it to
the Florida Shark Club of Jacksonville—
fifty of the finest, hardest-working sport fishermen
it has been my pleasure to know. Had they not
given me such an incurable case of shark fever,
the subject of this book would
not be what it is.

Contents

A TIME FOR TIGERS

Night Shark

Standing in knee-deep water on the sand bar at the mouth of Phillips Inlet, Shandy reeled hard but he couldn't feel anything on his line. Whatever had grabbed his bait and streaked into deep water must have broken the line and gotten away, taking his hook, leader, and lead as well. There was nothing left to do except reel in.

It had been hot when he waded to the bar and the sun had been in his eyes. The Gulf was choppy but the water was clear and blue and pleasant with the cool surge of the surf against his legs and the tingling swirl of sand against his feet. Now the sea was almost calm and the gentle swells mirrored the copper and gold of the setting sun. The rod was heavy in his shoulder harness and the palm of his hand smarted from cranking the big chrome reel. But a glance at the spool told him the line was almost in. He was watching for the end of it to come through the water when the tip of his rod suddenly bucked downward. And then he saw the shark.

It loomed surprisingly big and black against the bottom as it came straight toward him and stopped not six feet away. Shandy's heart pounded. He had never been that close to a big shark before. It looked eight feet long, maybe more. The shark swung its broad, blunt head from side to side trying to rid itself of the cable leader trailing from the corner of its mouth. It had not seen the boy yet and Shandy did not move a muscle.

Abruptly the shark turned and swam along the edge of the bar. Shandy quickly snapped the reel out of gear to give it line. He didn't intend to let the shark get away but he knew better than to make it mad while it was this close and still full of fight.

Line ticked off the spool. As the reel speeded up, Shandy's heart thumped one beat ahead of it. When the shark had taken about fifty yards of line, he lowered the tip of his rod, flicked the reel into gear, and hauled back hard—once . . . twice—driving the hook in solidly.

The shark lashed the water and made a long sizzling run to the east, paralleling the beach. Almost the whole 400 yards of heavy line were out before Shandy forced it to turn. Leaning back heavily in his harness and pulling with all his weight against the curved straining rod, he felt the change of direction as the shark smashed through the crest of a wave and reversed its course, heading back toward the west.

For the next half hour the boy waged a tug-of-war with the big shark. When it ran, it was all he could do to hang on and keep from being pulled off the sand bar. But when the shark paused, he started to haul and reel, gaining line until the shark turned and charged off on another tangent. Finally the runs were becoming shorter and gradually Shandy regained line until almost all of it was in. Almost all? That meant the shark was right in front of him again!

Sweat trickled down his face as he searched the dark water. There it was, farther to his left this time, lying motionless just beyond the edge of the bar. It was facing him and Shandy knew the shark saw him now. It wasn't fighting the hook any longer. It watched him with cold, menacing eyes. Shandy jerked the rod several times to get it to move away. The shark paused, then deliberately flicked its tail and swam into the shallow channel between the beach and the bar. The boy freewheeled the spool so nothing would hinder it. The line moved slowly down the slough to the east.

A slight breeze rippled the water. Shandy straightened his shoulders and let it blow under his leather harness, cooling his sweat-soaked skin. On the horizon the sun sank into the Gulf of Mexico.

It wouldn't be long before dark. Shandy wondered if he could fight the shark better from the beach. He had waded fifty yards from shore to reach the bar and since the tide was going out, the water in the slough would be less than waist deep. On the sand bar it only came up to the calves of his legs now and he was glad of that. He glanced toward the inlet. Through the pass on the other side of the highway bridge he could see the *Albatross,* Catfish Jackson's houseboat where his friend, Jib Woods, was helping the captain get supper. The line stopped moving off the reel. From its angle the shark was somewhere well out beyond the end of the slough. Shandy knew if he was ever going to get this over with he was going to have to do it from the beach.

He stepped off the sand bar and headed for shore. He hadn't gone six feet when the water churned and with a yelp he stumbled back up onto the bar as the shark shot past in front of him. Had he imagined it or had that crazy thing tried to attack him?

The shark must have doubled back, pulling the loose belly of line behind it. Shandy quickly reeled up slack to find out where the shark was. The line slanted to his left and about thirty feet away he barely could see the long dark shape lying motionless on the bottom, watching him. Shandy lifted the rod and yanked it viciously several times but the shark didn't move. Cautiously he stepped off the bar into deeper water. The shark darted forward and Shandy leaped back just as it rose half out of water and rammed head-on into the sand bar.

There wasn't any doubt about it now: the shark wanted him to try for the beach—it was baiting him! He moved a safer distance from the edge of the bar, then felt foolish for letting a fish get him in a spot like that. There had to be something he could do. The water was just above his ankles now. He knew it wouldn't drop much farther. But even at low tide there was plenty of water in the slough for the shark. And Shandy shivered as he remembered that when the tide came back in there would be plenty of water over the bar for the shark too.

He looked longingly toward the houseboat and wished it had not been too far away for him to attract attention. Lights were on in the cabin. When he didn't come after dark he knew that Catfish and Jib would start looking for him. But by then it might be too late.

Shandy slowly tightened his line. The shark came toward the bar, then cruised by in front of him, its black dorsal fin high out of water. When it reached the end of its tether it turned and made another pass, so close this time that its blunt snout gouged a furrow of sand at the edge of the bar. Then it swung back into the murky brown darkness of the slough.

Shandy wondered whether, if he cut the line, the shark would go away. But if he did cut it and the shark didn't leave, he'd have no way of knowing it. No, he would have to keep the line intact to tell where the shark was.

But maybe if he were to take all the drag off the line, to free-spool it, the shark might wander off far enough to give him time to get ashore. He felt the line. From the way it was moving the shark was patrolling slowly and deliberately back and forth between the bar and shore. Shandy took the reel out of gear and snapped off the clicker, letting the line go completely free. Then he waited.

The sea around him grew black and calm. In the distance he could see the warm glow of lights from St. Andrews. Watching it made him feel even colder. He forced his eyes back to the water in front of him. He strained hard to see something—anything, a movement— that it became an endless yawning black pit. He quickly looked up at the stars to keep from becoming dizzy.

The slight invisible tug of the current against his ankles told him the tide was still going out. But soon that would cease as the tide reached its ebb. Whatever he was going to do he had to do before it started back in. Suddenly something struck his foot. He jumped, frightening the school of minnows that had run into him. They slashed and pelted the water in a panic to get out of his way.

Fifteen minutes later he touched the arbor of his reel. Almost the entire 400 yards of line were gone! But how? Had the shark taken it? Or had the current only pulled a long loose loop in his line?

Shandy looked toward the beach and saw its faint white outline. The water between couldn't be much more than knee-deep. Maybe the shark had taken the line. The beach was only fifty yards away. He could cover that in nothing flat if . . .

He unsnapped the reel from his shoulder harness. Holding the rod high he squatted down, trying to silhouette the line against the distant glow of lights to see which way it was slanting. As far as he could tell it was going southeast toward the open Gulf.

Taking a bearing on the beach, Shandy clenched his teeth and jumped in, splashing through the water in leaps and bounds. Suddenly he tripped and sprawled forward, thrashing wildly as the gurgling blackness rolled over him. Gasping and sputtering, he jumped up and ran.

Once on the hard-packed sand beach, he coughed up the stinging salt water he had swallowed. When he finally caught his breath he turned to look at the sea. And that's when he realized he didn't have his rod. He had dropped it when he fell!

For an instant his mind was blank. Then he remembered the tackle bag he had laid beside a plank on the beach. He ran to it and fumbled for his flashlight. On the sloping shingle of sand between the water and the beach the bright beam fell on a loop of slack line that had washed up high and dry. He picked it up and drew it toward him. The line came easily at first, coiling in a loose pile at his feet. Then it stopped. He tugged but it wouldn't come. The reel was snagged.

He tried pulling in the other end of the line but there was a steady unyielding weight on it east of the slough. He turned his light out into the channel. Not more than six yards away he saw the faint gleam of the reel's chrome. It lay in a couple of feet of water on the edge of the drop-off into the channel. He could get it and still stay in shallow water.

Holding the light in front of him he ran for the reel. As he reached down and grasped the heavy rod, a glistening black shape suddenly rose in front of him—a lone wave smashed against him and left him shuddering in its frothy wake. He raced back to the beach. He was mad now, mad at himself for letting something like a wave panic him, and mad at the shark for causing him so much trouble in the first place.

He clipped his shoulder harness to the reel with a

vengeance. Quickly he reeled up his line until it tightened and slanted far out into the channel. Then he struck the rod with all his might.

Somewhere in the darkness beyond the bar came an instant response. He heard the water boil, then he was being dragged down the beach. He tried to lean back, to dig in his heels, but he couldn't. The brake on his reel smoked as line whisked through the guides. He cranked the big handle uselessly. But he was determined not to let the shark get the best of him this time. Before he realized it, he was up to his knees in the surf and his reel was almost empty. Then abruptly his bent rod sprang straight and Shandy would have sworn that he felt the exact moment when the line broke.

He started to reel in, then decided to do it on the beach. Just as he stepped ashore he thought he heard a thud and the breaking of a wave behind him. Grabbing his flashlight, he swept the beam over the channel just as the shark's fin slid underwater exactly where he had been standing.

Dropping the light he ran backward up the beach, rapidly turning the reel handle. When he had almost reached the dunes he sat down and jabbed the butt of the rod into the sand just as the tip bowed into its familiar arc. The shark was still on! Bracing the rod against his bent leg, he forced the handle around with both hands. There was a violent splashing at the edge of the channel. He urged it around again and again until he couldn't turn it another inch. From the smacking thuds that came from the water he knew exactly where the shark was now. It was grounded at the edge of the beach.

As he unsnapped himself from the rod a powerful beam of light speared the darkness behind him and he heard Jib's shrill whistle.

"Over here!" he yelled. "I just landed a shark!"

He caught the line in his hand and carefully followed it toward the water as the weaving spotlight and two running figures drew closer.

"Boy, am I glad to see you," said Shandy, trying to keep the shake out of his voice.

His pudgy friend skidded to a stop. "Gosh, we thought something had happened to you," panted Jib Woods.

"That's right," said Catfish. Flashing the light over Shandy as he came up, he added, "From the looks of you, something did."

"Look over here a minute," said Shandy. He led the way to the water's edge.

Catfish's light fell on the huge grayish-brown shark as it lay half in, half out of the water, still twitching its long, curved tail.

"Good golly!" he said.

"Did *you* catch that thing, Shandy?"

"Yeah—but boy, you don't know how close it was to being the other way around."

"No wonder you were late for supper," said the captain with a touch of awe in his voice. "That's the meanest-looking tiger shark I've seen in a long time."

"How can you tell he's a tiger?" asked Jib.

"Those stripes along his sides. There's just one kind of shark got marks like those and he's a killer."

"I'd sure like to get his jaws for a trophy," said Shandy. "Think we could pull him up on the beach with the leader?"

"Don't know why not," said the captain. "Let's give it a try."

The three of them took hold of the ten-foot plastic-covered cable that was attached to the hook deep in the shark's mouth. On Catfish's command they all heaved together, straining against the weight of the shark.

Slowly its big body slid up the sand incline. As it plowed over the edge into soft sand, the shark came to life.

"Look out!" yelled Catfish.

The shark arched its body and slammed the beach so hard Shandy felt the impact through the soles of his feet. Then, with jaws gaping, it swung its head wildly, each time snapping its jaws together with the hollow clack of jagged teeth.

"We gotta put a stop to that." Catfish searched the beach with his light, then picked up the plank near Shandy's tackle bag.

"Stand clear," he said.

While Jib held the light the captain swung the plank over his shoulder and brought it down hard on the shark's head. After two more blows the shark quivered and lay still.

Just as quickly, the captain took out his jackknife, leaned down and made a slashing movement with his arm.

"What are you doing?" asked Jib.

"Just a little surgery," said Catfish. "Tiger sharks are good at eating things that aren't good for them. The last one I opened had swallowed a roll of tarpaper, a man's overcoat, a ship's sextant, and a chicken coop."

"What a bellyache he must have had!"

"He probably did. . . . Feels like this one swallowed something he shouldn't have, too."

Catfish worked quickly. He slit open the shark's stomach and spilled out its contents.

Along with an assortment of fish that had been the shark's last meal was a hard, bright yellow object the size and shape of a grapefruit. Two short metal prongs protruded from it. Catfish carried it to the water and rinsed it off.

"It's a float from a seine net, isn't it?"

"Too heavy for that," said Catfish. "Might be something off a boat. Maybe it's a Navy instrument of some kind."

"But how would a shark get ahold of that?"

Catfish shrugged. "Beats me." He handed it to Shandy. "There's no marking on it."

"Whatever it is, the outside is made of plastic," said Shandy, thumping it with his knuckle. "And it's hollow."

"If it's something that belongs to the Navy, I reckon they'd be glad to get it back again. Maybe we'd better run it in to Saint Andrews tomorrow and let Kip Norden take a look at it," suggested Catfish.

"Who's Kip Norden?" asked Shandy.

"An oceanographer friend of mine. You'll like him."

"An ocean—what?" questioned Jib.

"Oceanographer," Catfish repeated slowly. "That's a man who studies about the geography of the ocean and all the things in it. Kip's head of a Naval research outfit that's studying the Gulf. If anyone can tell us what that thing is, Kip can."

Shandy could not have explained it, but as he examined the strange yellow ball in his hands he felt the same tingle of excitement he had felt when he had found the treasure map scratched on the old telescope from Uncle Martin's sea chest. That map had led them into some dangerous adventures before they had discovered its secret. But that had been last summer when he was only twelve and Jib was only ten. They hadn't done so badly then, when they solved the mystery of Mound Key, and they were a year older now.

Was there a mystery connected with this yellow ball that was constructed with such precision? And would it lead them into more dangerous adventures? A shiver of anticipation ran through Shandy. Whatever lay ahead, he knew that he and Jib were ready.

Strange Current

The next morning, as the three of them waited to see Mr. Norden at the Naval Research Bureau in St. Andrews, Shandy felt uneasy. He surveyed the room with a cautious eye. The outer office had an official look to it. A row of folding chairs where they were sitting occupied one end of the long, cypress-paneled room. On the wall behind them was an orderly row of black-framed photographs showing various naval work boats in operation; also two aerial photographs of offshore research towers. They were marked in large white letters "Stage I" and "Stage II." Shandy had seen the towers, but in the pictures they looked different. When you were in a boat offshore they looked something like giant toadstools. But they were really buildings on platforms supported by tall steel pilings that held them fifty feet out of water. All he knew about them was that boats weren't allowed to tie up to the pilings to fish.

Opposite them, the lady who had told them to wait while Mr. Norden was on the telephone continued with her typing. On the wall behind her was a picture of the President of the United States. To her left were several · enclosed offices where other typewriters were faintly clicking. Everything about the front of the bureau seemed very formal and proper, but as Shandy glanced curiously up the hall to its far end, he noticed a gradual change. The framed photographs gave way to unframed maps of all sizes with colored pins sticking in them. The last map wasn't even on the wall, it was hanging halfway off a temporary-looking drawing board propped on two sawhorses. On the floor beneath it were the unmistakable yellow tanks and chrome regulator of a scuba rig. The diving gear lay beside several big bottles of clear liquid, some of which had dead fish floating in them.

Occasionally a man in a white uniform came out of one office with a stack of papers and went into another. And then Shandy realized why he felt uneasy. The bureau reminded him vaguely of a hospital—in fact, it even smelled a little like one. Although he wasn't too eager to dwell on the circumstances of his last trip to a hospital, Shandy would never forget the old Japanese diving helmet he and Jib had found in his uncle's old sea chest. The solid-brass dome-shaped diving headgear was badly banged up and didn't have any glass in it, but Jib had thought it would make a swell space helmet. The trouble was, once Shandy tried it on he couldn't get it off. Failing to pry it off, Jib had even smeared him with a pound of butter to make him slippery, but he couldn't get his chin past a big dent in the collar. After that it was one long nightmare, with a wild ride to the hospital where not even the doctors and nurses could figure out how to get it off, before the police finally came and sawed it off.

A buzzer sounded.

Shandy snapped out of his reverie and ran a hand over his wet brow.

The lady at the desk smiled and nodded to them.

"Mr. Norden will see you now. Last office on the left."

As they went down the hall, Shandy wondered whether Kip Norden would look like a doctor.

The door to the office was open. When they went in, Shandy was pleasantly surprised. Mr. Norden wore white sneakers and khakis instead of a white uniform, and he acted as if he had known them all his life. He was a tall, suntanned man with sandy brown hair and bright blue eyes. The first thing he told the boys was to call him Kip, which was for his friends; the "Mr.," he said, was for the Navy. The next thing he said was, "Where'd you get that piece of equipment, Captain? Out of the belly of a shark?"

Catfish almost bit off the stem of his corncob pipe.

"How in tarnation did you know that?"

Kip smiled wryly. "It's been one of my pet headaches." He took their find and examined it more closely.

"I told the boys it was some kind of Navy gadget."

"Nope," said Kip. "Not ours."

Catfish frowned. "Then whose is it?"

"Frankly, we don't know, Captain."

"Do you have any idea what it is?" asked Shandy.

"Basically it's something we call a sensor—an electronic radio sensor," said Kip. "We use similar underwater instruments at our fixed offshore stations for monitoring such things as water temperatures, salinity, currents, tides. The information is automatically radioed by the sensor to a receiving unit on the surface, telemetered ashore, then fed into a computer for evaluation." Kip held the small yellow sphere with the tips of his fingers and slowly revolved it, studying its smooth surface thoughtfully.

"The interesting aspect of this item is that it doesn't seem to have been designed for sensing any of these things. All it contains is an ultra-low-frequency signal

transmitter, the sensing unit, and a battery which pro-
vides power as long as these probes"—he touched the two
metallic prongs projecting from the sphere—"are immersed
in acid." Kip shrugged. "The rest of it is empty space. The
case is maybe three or four times bigger than it need be to
house those miniaturized components." Kip glanced up
with an apologetic smile, suddenly aware that they might
not understand any of what he was talking about.

"What I'd like to know," pursued Jib intently, "is how
you knew we got it from a shark. You weren't there when
Shandy landed him."

"Right you are." Kip Norden's eyes danced. "I'm a mind-
reader, Jib. What's more, I'll bet you a chocolate soda that
you took it out of the stomach of a tiger shark."

Jib almost fell off his chair in surprise.

Kip laughed. "That really wasn't fair of me," he said,
hastening to explain. "You see, Jib, this isn't the first one
of these things that's been found." He got up from his
desk and walked over to a large geodetic map of the Gulf
of Mexico. He pointed at the map. "Last spring three of
them turned up between here—Pascagoula, Mississippi—
and here—Cape San Blas, Florida. Early this summer,
two more were picked up by shrimpers in the DeSoto
Canyon area." He indicated a spot offshore. "The two
things we do know," Kip said, turning back to face them,
"are that all of the sensors came from sharks caught along
this coast and all of those sharks were tigers."

Catfish scratched his head. "I've heard of sharks eating
some pretty peculiar things, but this sensor business beats
me."

"You're not the only one, Captain. The Navy's getting a
little beat trying to figure it out too. Since our department
is mainly interested in the Eastern Gulf, where these
underwater unidentified floating objects have been show-

ing up, Washington has given us the job of finding out what they are and where they're coming from." Kip paused. "There's nothing classified about all this—at least not yet—but you understand, Captain, I don't want any newspaper publicity. If they got hold of it, these mystery balls of ours might become as popular with the public as flying saucers. And that I don't need."

Catfish nodded. "I know what you mean, Kip. We'll keep it quiet, won't we, boys?"

"Yes sir," spoke up Shandy, and Jib added quickly, "We won't tell anybody."

"Well, I guess that's that." Catfish got up to go. "Sure wish there was some way we could help you, Kip."

"You and me both," smiled the Navy man as he reached out to shake hands. Then he paused, and a frown wrinkled his brow. "Are you serious?" he asked Catfish.

"What? About helping? Sure."

Kip sat down thoughtfully on the edge of his desk. "Didn't you tell me once that you skippered a commercial shark-fishing boat during World War II?"

"Yep. Right here out of Saint Andrews. The government needed shark livers to make vitamin A, so we caught sharks."

"And when they learned how to synthesize vitamin A, that knocked the bottom out of the shark-fishing business?"

"It sure did," said Catfish. "We sold the boat and hired out to net shrimp on shares. My old crew's still working a shrimp boat out of Panama City."

"Think they'd be interested in going after sharks again at a better salary?"

Catfish didn't have to think twice before answering. "Darn tootin' they would—they'd jump at the chance. Why?"

Kip picked up the sensor. "Our UFO here is reason number one," he said. "At the rate we've been going, it looks as if the only way we're going to get any real information about these things is to do some backtracking —catch more sharks with sensors until they lead us to their source. It's taken us a month to equip a trawler just for that purpose. All we lack now is a crew that knows how to handle sharks."

"They know how to do that, all right," said Catfish. "But finding the right sharks could mean covering an awful lot of territory."

"Maybe and maybe not," said Kip. "We've got some leads that might pay off sooner than you think. Want to take time to hear the whole story?"

"You bet we do," said Catfish.

"Yes sir," said Shandy and Jib eagerly.

"Okay," said Kip. "Two years ago one of our big research vessels, the *R/V Oregon*, finished up a seven-year study of the eastern Gulf of Mexico. Specifically what they were hunting was sufficient tuna to support a brand new eastern Gulf fishery that would put the poor shrimp fishermen in ports like Pascagoula and Panama City into a more profitable business. The *Oregon* found the tuna all right, enough to support a tremendous fishery. They also stumbled onto something they hadn't expected—large concentrations of sport fish: marlin, broadbill swordfish, wahoo, sailfish; ocean-going fish that nobody even knew were in the Gulf, let alone as close to shore as some were.

"That's how I got into the picture two years ago," Kip continued. "The Bureau of Naval Research and the U. S. Fisheries Department sent me down here to make an extensive study of these waters to find out among other things why the fish were here and how large the population might be. To make a long story short, we found that these fish were coming out of the Caribbean in a peculiar flow of water called the Yucatan Current. The physical differences of this current kept it from mixing with the other water of the Gulf. Because of these differences, the fish we were interested in stayed in it, the same way you would stay in a hallway or corridor. Anyway, our drift-bottle program revealed that each spring this current cuts northward across the Gulf of Mexico until it intersects the outflowing waters of the Mississippi River. When this happens the current is deflected or bounced to the east where it skirts our northwest coast of Florida. Then just off Cape San Blas it swings into a big circle that centers off a deep bottom depression known as the DeSoto Canyon. The whole system holds up like this for about six months, then as the pressures of the current become less, it breaks down and the fish follow it back to the Caribbean or out through the Florida Straits and up the east coast with the Gulf Stream."

"Well I'll be—!" exclaimed Catfish.

"Now here's the interesting part," said Kip. "Our tests have shown that this current concentrates itself, and so do the fish in it. One week it may be only five miles wide and the next it might be fifteen miles wide. This means that the chances of catching these fish are far better when the current is narrow and compressed. We know, for example, that one of these compressions will occur this week in the DeSoto Canyon area."

"But how will this affect our sharks?" asked Catfish.

"According to my records and charts, all seven of the sensor-carrying sharks we have caught came from this current during the peak compression periods. The same thing that brought that snow-white beach out there—sand we have identified as coming from the bottom of the Caribbean—brought your tiger shark ashore. The expand-

ing current literally pushed it in. And Shandy was fortu-
nate enough to catch it. I think that with commercial
longline fishing rigs and some electronic tracking gear
we've rigged up to pick up signals from the sensors, we
won't have too much trouble locating the sharks we're
after. And anyway it'll give me a chance to tag and release
a few of the other sharks for a scientist friend of mine up
at the Sandy Hook research station."

When Kip finished, Catfish heaved a sigh and lit his
corncob pipe. "That's really something," he said, "figuring
out all that." He sucked on his pipe thoughtfully. "If those
sharks are coming out of the Caribbean . . . maybe
that's where they're picking up those sensors."

"We thought of that," said Kip. "The Navy checked out
every commercial shark-fishing interest they knew of
down there. Not one reported finding any sensors."

"Then they're getting them between here and there."

"Possibly," said Kip. "Here's something else I learned
last week in Washington. It seems that the only people in
the world making use of the information we got from the
Oregon reports are the Japanese, Russians, and Caribans.
The Japanese are presently putting Gulf tuna on the
world market through canneries in Puerto Rico. And a
little less than six months ago Cariba stepped up the
number of oceanographic vessels operating from their
island. These ships are enormous floating laboratories
loaded with the latest scientific equipment to study everything there is to learn about the sea. Now there may be no
connection between those ships and our sharks, but we do
know those people are extremely interested in something
going on out there in the Gulf. Of course," he added, "it
may only be those tuna."

"Gosh, is it legal for them to do that?" asked Shandy. "I

mean, having their ships out there and taking fish we discovered."

"I'm afraid it is," said Kip, "as long as they stay beyond our territorial limits, which is three marine leagues or about twelve miles from shore."

"That's what we call the twelve-mile limit," said Catfish. "Some countries claim a lot more than that and if you get caught fishing in their waters they can give you trouble."

Kip turned to Catfish. "Anyway, that's the picture, Captain. As I said, we've got a trawler rigged for tracking sensors and outfitted for catching sharks. She's the *R/V Elmira* and she's at your disposal."

Catfish looked up. "At *my* disposal?"

"Sure. You wouldn't want that shark-fishing crew of yours to go off without a skipper, would you?"

"Well now . . . well, I . . ."

"Go ahead," urged Shandy. "You can do it, Catfish!"

"It would only be for three, maybe four, days at a trip, then you could come back for a breather. With you handling the ship and the fishing gear and me on the electronic equipment, we can't lose."

"Well, by golly," mused Catfish, "I gotta admit I'd get a kick out of shark fishing with the old crew again."

"Say yes!" insisted Jib and Shandy.

"Okay, I will." The captain's eyes twinkled. "On one condition, Kip."

"Name it."

"That the boys here go along with us."

"Certainly," said Kip without an instant's hesitation. "You didn't think we'd leave behind our prize shark catchers, did you?" The Navy man's face was completely serious.

"Goll-y, did you hear that, Shandy?"

"I sure did!" Shandy gasped. "And he isn't fooling!"

"Gosh, when could we go?"

"It's up to the captain," said Kip. "There's nothing to take aboard but the crew and ourselves. We could push off tomorrow if they were ready."

"Ready?" said Catfish. "Why those fellas would have their gear aboard and be ready for sharks about two shakes after I got word to them."

"Fine. Tell them it's the R/V Elmira. She's moored at the city pier." Kip turned to the boys. "You fellas don't think your folks will mind the Navy borrowing you for a couple of days, do you?"

"Shoot-a-mighty no!" piped up Jib. "We went off on a trip to Mound Key with Catfish in his houseboat last summer and worse things happened to us than that."

Kip chuckled. "Seems I do remember reading something about your adventures on the Albatross in the newspapers." He winked at Catfish.

"Compared to that, my Aunt Tilou will think this is tame," added Shandy.

"Good, then it's settled," said Kip. "Round up your crew, Captain, and I'll see all of you on board ship tomorrow morning at oh-six hundred."

Elmira and Crew

As the captain and the boys walked out on the fog-shrouded city pier shortly after sunrise the next morning they got their first look at the *R/V Elmira*. It was a sixty-foot, steel-gray, heavily painted trawler. The fog was lifting from the bay but it seemed unwilling to leave the squat, tired-looking boat that hugged close to the pilings. Her rails were dripping and her decks were glistening. A steady stream of water spewed from a starboard vent and some-where below decks a gas-driven bilge pump chugged reluctantly. Shandy shivered and turned up the collar of his windbreaker.

Kip Norden leaned out of the pilothouse perched over the forecastle and waved to them.

"C'mon aboard, fellas. We're about ready to shove off."

He met them on deck as they stepped over from the pier. There was a broad grin on his face.

"Captain, I don't know where you found that crew of yours but they took over here as if they'd been shipping out on the *Elmira* every day of their lives." He shook his head. "I keep expecting them to run up the skull and crossbones at any minute though."

Catfish chuckled and thumbed up the much laundered

and therefore bedraggled bill of his lucky swordfish cap, a permanent part of his sea-going uniform that not only served to shield his freckled head from the ravages of sun and sea, but, he was convinced, never failed to lead him to fish. The same was true of his belt, a very wide leather belt with a cherished brass buckle. The belt was too wide for the loops of his khaki pants so he merely strapped it around his waist on the outside. The round buckle was never dull, particularly the words embossed there—*Gott Mit Uns*. Catfish told the boys he had "liberated" it from the commander of a German submarine who had tried to sink his ship during World War I. Unlike the cap, which didn't always make it, the belt was worn with anything and everything from his Sunday suit to the overstretched top of his bulky boxer swimming trunks.

"The crew's not much to look at," said Catfish, "but they sure know their business. What're they up to now?"

"Well, your bearded friend's in the pilothouse getting the marine weather forecast. Jonah's sharpening hooks in the forecastle, and I think your engineer hollered something to me in Mexican about changing an oil filter before disappearing down the engine hatch some time ago—at least that's the way Big Clyde interpreted it. Sorry's in the galley where he left strict orders for you to report for some of the 'Navy's sorry coffee' the minute you came aboard," Kip said and laughed.

Catfish wagged his head indulgently. "Well, knowing Sorry, I reckon he's one cook we better not keep waiting. Let's go see what he's got to offer."

They made their way forward past the big deck winch and the tall midship booms; up the sloping deck and into the narrow galley where a lanky man with a flour sack tucked into the top of his rolled-up pants was banging pots and pans around in a locker under the gas stove.

As they came in he snapped erect. "Figured it wush about time for you to show up, Cap'n. Got your coffee good an' hot for ya."

Catfish introduced the boys to Sorry the cook.

"Pleesh t'meetsha," said Sorry, wiping his hands on his flour sack and greeting them with a grip that bulged the ropy sinews of his lanky arm. He was a skinny, chinless man with a sharp beaklike nose long enough for two. His skin was so white that Shandy wondered if he had ever been exposed to the sun. What hair he had was a close-cropped red fuzz with a bare spot the size of a small pancake on top. He wore a tight, colorfully stained T-shirt, baggy faded blue denims, and laceless canvas sneakers with their toes cut out. All items looked as if they belonged to someone else.

The first time the cook grinned at them Shandy would have sworn he didn't have teeth. But when he jumped back to the stove for the coffee pot, then turned around and grinned again—he had all of his teeth.

With studied care, Catfish puckered his brow and sipped a steaming mug of the cook's brew. His eyes clamped tight shut. His cheeks, stubbled with white whiskers he purposely had not shaved off the night before, began to pump like bellows.

The boys watched in fascination.

The cook stood by anxiously.

Catfish stretched out the tasting ritual as long as he dared, then his Adam's apple bounced, his lips smacked, and his eyes popped open.

"Sorry, I swear that's the best blamed cup of coffee you ever turned out!"

The lanky seaman looked crestfallen but the boys knew he was only fooling. He was really very pleased with the captain's compliment, although you wouldn't know it by the way he talked.

"It tastes like bilge water," he complained. "Sorriest I ever brewed." He poured a cup for Kip. "Same thing is wrong with that pot there that's wrong with the rest of this galley." He poured himself a cup. "Too blasted clean!" He took two hasty swallows. "Whole place is pretty sorry." He flourished a hand around his galley. "Coffee pots gotta be left alone to season up good before they give out proper coffee—same as an old iron frying pan. How's a body expect a body to fix proper grub in a galley that's so spic 'n' span ya don't dare touch nothin'?" He shrugged and turned back to his stove, muttering. "This's gonna be a pretty sorry trip if I don't get this galley shaped up," he promised darkly.

"Awww shoot, Sorry, don't worry none about that," said Catfish encouragingly. "You'll get it shaped up all right, I can count on that." The captain winked at Shandy and Jib. Kip in the meantime was seeking refuge behind his uptilted white mug, drinking his coffee fast but short of shaking all over while he was doing it.

It looked as if the men were going to stay in the galley and talk while the cook urged more of his "sorry" coffee on them, so Shandy and Jib quietly slipped out the door to explore the trawler on their own.

When they were by themselves on deck, Shandy said with a grin, "Boy, what'd you think of *him?*"

"I liked him. He kept running down his own coffee, but did you notice how he was eating up everything the captain said about it?" CO. SCHOOLS

"Sure did," said Shandy, smiling. C693527

Jib stepped over to the railing, leaned his back against it, and ran an appraising eye over the trawler.

"Have you ever seen a boat built crazier?" he laughed.

"What do you mean?"

"Well, look at it. It's built like one of those lopsided fun houses you see at carnivals. Everything's crooked. I'll bet there isn't a straight line in this whole boat."

Shandy joined his friend. He looked forward, then aft, and he saw exactly what Jib meant. The deck sloped steeply to the high bow; the pilothouse curved; the roof of the deckhouse sagged like the midship deck, then rose at the stern; the window frames were at all angles, no two alike; the door frames slanted and tilted to match the dip of the deck; and, now that he thought about it, everything in the galley had been constructed just as crazily.

"You're right," he said. "Why do you suppose they built it like that?"

Jib could see only one reason for it. "They probably made a mistake when they started and one mistake led to another. Like the sailboat we built that sank when we launched it."

"Yeah, but that was because we used warped boards."

"See? That's what I mean."

Jib might not be right, but until a better explanation came along Shandy figured that warped boards were as good a reason as any.

Jib was looking up at the pilothouse, which was reached by a narrow ladder with salt-encrusted iron railings. "Shall we start up there?" he asked.

"Let's check out the engine room first," said Shandy. "She'll be under way pretty soon, then we can go topside when we head out through the jetties."

"Good idea."

The boys made their way aft down the gradually sloping deck until they reached the rear of the low deckhouse. Once there, what momentarily claimed their attention was a magnificent power winch with three drums. It was marked with the name "Stroudsburg" and was much larger than the one Catfish had mounted ahead of the wheelhouse of the *Albatross*.

"This must be what they use for hauling in the shrimp nets," said Shandy. "It probably hooks up so the boat's engine drives it."

Jib was staring up at the steel boom attached to the towering mast and extending to the stern of the trawler. Two other booms angled off from the base of the mast on either side, and steel-cabled guy lines supported everything at the port and starboard bulkheads.

"Where's the nets?" Jib asked.

Shandy looked around but he didn't see any. "Beats me. Maybe she doesn't have any."

"Any shrimp boat I ever saw had nets," said Jib. "Heavy trawl nets."

"Yeah, but don't forget Kip said this was a converted trawler. If she doesn't go after shrimp any more they probably don't use them all the time."

"Maybe not." Jib walked aft toward the stern and peered down through a large deck hatch that had been left partway open. Normally it would have been the shrimp hold. Now the boys saw that it had been turned into a comfortable cabin. They got down on their knees and surveyed the spacious living quarters below decks. The companionway had a wide ladder leading down to the cabin. There were double bunks on the port and starboard sides with tall gray lockers at each end of them. Both bulkheads had several round brass portholes to let in light. A long green table divided the cabin up the middle and on each side of it were four dark green captain's chairs spaced so evenly the boys knew they had to be attached to the deck. By craning their necks they could see a man's legs through a doorway at the far end of the cabin, but since they were practically standing on their heads to see that much, they couldn't tell what he was doing.

Shandy finally straightened up. "C'mon," he said, "let's go down to the engine room."

"How do we get there?"

"Over there, I think." He pointed to a narrow companionway half hidden behind the winch. Jib followed him over to investigate it.

The opening was just large enough for a man to get through. A steep ladder led downward into the hold. As they looked in, a gust of warm air touched their faces carrying with it the oily smell of diesel fuel, fresh paint, and the faint, metallic odor of machinery. The rhythmic chugging of the bilge pump was louder now.

Without hesitating they climbed through the hatch and down the ladder. At the bottom they found themselves in a large room flanked by four great fuel-storage tanks. Built or squeezed into every available inch of space between them were a work bench, storage batteries, bilge pump, generator, and other equipment. Electric lights with wire-mesh covers dimly illuminated everything. Sitting squarely in the middle of the room was the engine. And what an engine! It was painted bright orange. The boys were so awed by its size that they almost fell over each other when a face with owlish eyes suddenly popped out from behind it and grinned at them.

"Hiya!" it said.

The boys gulped. "Hi! Who are you?"

"Chief engineer Rooster," the face explained cheerfully enough, neither coming out into full view nor retiring from sight.

All the boys could see was that Rooster had two enormous black eyes and white tufts of something in his curly black hair. The head bobbed slightly and the boys thought at first that it was going to duck back out of sight. Then they realized that the chief engineer was working on something with his hands at the other end of the engine.

"What are you doing back there?" Jib asked.

Rooster gritted his teeth, bobbed his head a final time, then scrambled out from behind his engine.

"Changing an oil filter." His prominent white teeth flashed as Rooster came into the light where they could see him better. He was a wiry little man in a pair of faded khaki pants, or half pants. The pant legs had been torn off two inches above his knobby knees. Except for a pair of ragged sneakers the only other thing he wore was a heavy coat of black oil and grease, smeared up his arms and splotched haphazardly around the rest of his anatomy. This accounted for his owlish black eyes which he had apparently rubbed once or twice.

"Filthiest filter I ever saw," said the chief engineer with a shake of his head. Like a man about to unveil a statue, the little Mexican dramatically reached out and started the diesel. As it vibrated into life, everything vibrated with it.

Rooster cocked his head and listened. The orange engine idled with a contented hum.

The tune it sang obviously satisfied him. "Fine engine now," he said, giving the big diesel an affectionate thump with the handle of his screwdriver. "She run like one hot tamale."

The boys weren't certain what he meant by that but they guessed it was good.

The chief engineer mopped himself half clean with a big wad of cotton waste, which explained the white tufts in his hair, then he grabbed a blower tube clipped to the bulkhead and called up to the bridge. When a muffled voice answered he asked who was speaking.

An explosive volley of words came through the tube. The chief engineer held the mouthpiece away from his ear and grinned delightedly.

When the racket ceased, he spoke into the tube again.

"This is chief engineer Rooster speaking from the engine room," he announced smoothly. "When you get ready to go up there it's okaydoky with me, Big Cheese." Then he immediately clamped the crude telephone back into its holder and jumped away from it with a mischievous snicker as if expecting it to spit fire and belch smoke. It didn't, but there was another blistering verbal volley from the bridge.

"That Big Clyde guy sure knows some words," the chief engineer said with admiration. "Don't talk much but when he does they come out like chili peppers." The little Mexican popped his grease-rimmed eyes and blew on his fingers and the boys doubled up with laughter.

There were sounds of movement on the deck overhead. Rooster and the man in the pilothouse exchanged some more words through the tube, then Rooster fluttered around his huge orange engine and things began to happen. The big diesel cleared its throat and hummed a different tune. The trawler shuddered and moved. The boys felt the heavy throbbing vibrations through the soles of their shoes. The tune stopped and changed pitch. Rooster flapped his arms amid the machinery like the director of a symphony orchestra. The diesel shifted into another octave, then as the sound gradually increased the boys sensed the motion and knew the trawler was feeling its way out of the marina and into the bay.

When Rooster paused for a breather Shandy asked, "How big an engine is that?"

"She got three hundred horses," Rooster reported proudly.

"It sure must take a lot of fuel oil," said Jib, looking at the large storage tanks.

Rooster shrugged. "There no filling stations where we going."

"How much are we carrying?" asked Shandy.

"Sixteen hundred gallon. 'Nough to make this boat go two thousand mile without refueling."

The boys whistled under their breaths.

"Hey!" Rooster exclaimed suddenly. "You see my fishing pole upstairs?"

Jib shook his head. "We didn't see any rods at all."

"Aw, I don't mean those toothpicks—they stowed forward someplace. I mean *mine*—the big one—up on deck near where you come down here."

"The winch?"

"Sure, what you think?" beamed the little Mexican. "I catch sharks maybe five, six at a time with that rig."

The boys didn't know whether to believe him or not.

"I sure want to see that," said Shandy.

Rooster winked. "You wait. You will."

Kip's Electronic Shark Hunter

The *Elmira* was turning out of the bay and moving up the channel toward the jetties when the boys climbed out of the engine room and went forward.

On the port side near the galley they passed a large wooden box they had failed to investigate.

"What do you suppose they keep in there?" asked Jib curiously.

"Open it and see."

Jib unfastened the latches and lifted the lid. As he looked in his eyes widened.

"Well, what d'ya know about that!" he exclaimed.

Shandy glanced over his shoulder. The box shielded a stainless-steel freezer loaded with food on one side and boxes of frozen baitfish on the other. Jib wasn't looking at the baitfish.

"Okay," murmured Shandy, somewhat annoyed by his pudgy friend's rapt fascination with the contents of the freezer. "Now that you know where it is, let's go see if there's anybody we know on the jetties."

Reluctantly Jib forced his eyes away from a stack of frozen T-bone steaks and carefully closed the box.

From the trawler's starboard bow they had a good view

of the long tar-topped jumble of broken rock that flanked the west side of the channel and reached out from the sugar white beaches into the Gulf of Mexico. Opposite it on the east side was a similar rock jetty. Both protected the mouth of the channel and, as the boys well knew, were mighty fine places to fish. The channel was deep here and the currents were frequently swift. In the spring, large schools of cobia raced in and out of the pass, their long dark bodies looking more like sharks than the edible gamefish they were. And to stand barefoot on one of the slippery big rocks at the point of the jetty with the waves breaking against your knees, a deeply arced Calcutta rod belting you in the stomach while a fifty-pound fighting-mad cobia smashed and battered his way out to sea with your line strumming tighter than a guitar string—well that, Shandy and Jib had to admit, was nothing short of sheer delight. The jetties to them meant cobia in the spring; hardtail, sharks, and catfish in the summer; mackerel, whiting, and kings in the fall; bluefish, redfish, and trout in the winter; not to mention all the other species that swept through the pass sometime during the year—the pompano, big rays, black drum, flounder, sheepshead, schools of mullet so thick they blackened the green water like a thunderhead. The jetties attracted fish and the fish attracted armies of fishermen—few of whom knew the tricks of fishing the rocky escarpment. Consequently Shandy and Jib frequently did a booming business in the summer diving up lost lures with their scuba gear and reselling their salvage at half price on a first-come, first-served basis. No pile of rocks had ever given two boys more fun and more profit than the St. Andrews jetties had given Shandy and Jib. But at the moment they weren't missing it in the least.

"The hardtail must be running," said Shandy, cupping

his hands over his eyes as he studied clumps and clusters of anglers crowding the jetty and rapidly whipping light-weight spinning rods in the air.

"Bet those rocks are covered with lures already," said Jib.

"There's nobody diving either," said Shandy.

Jib watched in silence. After a while he said, "You don't suppose a school of pompano came in, do you?"

"No—it must be hardtail. They'd be fishing harder if it was pompano."

"Maybe the lures will still be there when we get back," said Jib.

"Yeah, maybe they will," said Shandy. But both knew they wouldn't. Other divers would get them. When they came back the fish would be gone and so would the lures. But there would be another time.

"I'd still rather be here than there, wouldn't you, Shandy?"

"You bet I would," said Shandy. And he meant it.

As the trawler nosed out into the Gulf, its steep bow dipped and rose over the humps and valleys of incoming waves. The water was cleaner and clearer now and even the sky seemed bluer with only a few fleecy cotton candy clouds fluffed up on the horizon. The horizon, however, was lifting and falling, tilting and turning in such a way that it wasn't long before Jib's stomach was doing the same thing.

His hands tightened on the railing. "I'm beginning to feel not so good," he said in a low voice.

Shandy glanced up, worried. His friend's face had lost its ruddy glow and was turning white.

"Hang on, Jib. It'll be better farther out as soon as we get away from the pass."

Jib swallowed uncertainly. "I . . . I know," he managed through clenched teeth, "—if this crazy boat doesn't roll over before that."

"Try to keep your mind off it. Look at something steady. Look at the horizon."

"Thanks," murmured Jib. "That's my trouble."

"Want to go below and lie down?"

Jib shook his head bravely. "Uh-uh. I-I'll be okay." He closed his eyes for a second but that made his stomach churn more. He clenched the railing more determinedly than ever. A light sweat popped out on his forehead.

Shandy knew he had to do something to get his friend's mind off the boat's motion. Something, anything—and fast.

"C'mon with me," he said.

"Where to?"

"Over there—the forecastle. I want to see where we're bunking."

When they came to the open deck hatch just ahead of the pilothouse, Jib said stubbornly, "I'm not going down there."

"You don't have to. If we lie down we can see every- thing from here."

Jib groaned but he did as Shandy suggested. Flat on their stomachs they looked through the two-foot-wide opening into what was the crew's quarters. It was a triangular compartment built in the bow of the trawler. There were four berths, two on each side; a large locker, and a head. Behind the ladder a door opened aft into the engine compartment.

As the boys peered into the forecastle, a powerfully built seaman, tanned the color of well-oiled saddle leather, glanced up.

"C'mon down." The man smiled good-naturedly.

"Thanks. We're just looking," said Shandy.

Everything about the man was large, his feet, his hands, his muscles—even the broad, sharply chiseled features of his face. He was sitting on the edge of one of the lower bunks in a loose-fitting white shirt and pants that emphasized his tan. There was a sheath knife on his belt which Shandy noticed was braided rope; his shirt sleeves were rolled tightly around his bulging biceps; and his big calloused bare feet were planted firmly on the deck like sections of railroad track. He was sharpening hooks with a steel file but they were the largest hooks either of the boys had ever seen. Each one was as thick as a pencil and longer than a man's hand. The curve between the shank and the barb was so big it would encircle a man's wrist without touching either side; and there must have been fifty of them lined up like question marks along the rail of the berth opposite the seaman.

With a final rasp to the barb of a hook he was working on, the man hung it with the others and looked up at the boys again.

"You friends of the captain, I bet."

"Yes sir." Shandy and Jib introduced themselves.

"Good to know you. I'm Jonah." With a grin he nodded toward the row of hooks that jangled every time the trawler rolled. "You think we catch anything with those things?"

"We should. They look big enough to catch a whale," said Jib.

"I've used shark hooks before but nothing that size," said Shandy.

"These are special kind of longline hook," Jonah explained. "Big so we can unhook sharks fast and rebait in a hurry."

"But why is the upper part of the hook—the shank—bent in like that?"

"That's so when the shark chomps down on the bait he hooks himself—and stays hooked too."

Jonah's hooks suddenly clattered together loudly as the bow rose steeply, then dropped with a shuddering crash into a deep wave trough. The boys clutched the tilted foredeck but below, in the forecastle, Jonah still sat perched on the edge of the berth where he hadn't moved a muscle, as if he were part of the boat itself.

"This thing sure rolls a lot," Jib commented through clenched teeth.

"Shrimp boats always roll. Round bottom. Best seaworthy boat there is," said Jonah. "You get used to it."

Shandy asked Jib if he was feeling any better.

Jib nodded. "A little, I guess . . . but not much."

Someone hailed them from amidships. It was Catfish. They waved and scrambled aft. When they reached him he had walked to the stern to toss a slice of bread to a flock of sea gulls that swooped and dove over the boiling wake of the big trawler. Overhead the booms creaked and groaned against their fastenings.

"Have you been in the pilothouse yet?" Catfish asked.

"We were going but we haven't made it yet, Captain."

"Good, let's go up then. Kip wants to show you some of our radio gear."

As they passed the engine room, Rooster stuck his head out of the hatch and called to them.

"*Qué tal, Capitán?*" he yelled over the whirring roar of his engine. His eyes were still black and bits of lint were still scattered through his hair. An oilcan with a long spout was in his hand.

"Hello, Rooster!" Catfish greeted him warmly. "How goes it yourself? What are you doing down there?"

"Just oiling her up a little, *Capitán*. She's turning out pretty good *ahree-pee-emays*, no?"

"Sounds fine," smiled Catfish.

"Huh?" The little Mexican cupped his ear.

"I said," shouted Catfish, "your r.p.m.'s sound fine!"

The chief engineer nodded and giggled, then dropped back into his hole again. Through the narrow hatch Shandy and Jib saw him crouched over his machinery with the oilcan, furiously squirting everything that moved.

Catfish chuckled as they went forward. "You'd never know he was a reformed safecracker, would you?"

"A safecracker!"

"So he says." Catfish laughed. "Claims he gave it up when he decided it was a lot safer cranking engines than cracking safes. Of course he won't admit it in so many words, but he lets you know the profession will never be the same without him."

They climbed the ladder to the pilothouse.

As they went in, Kip looked up from some charts. "Welcome to the brain box, boys. What do you think of the boat?"

"It's swell," said Shandy. "This is the first time I ever saw one with the pilothouse up on top."

"Not much like the other Gulf shrimpers, is it?" Kip said with a grin. "We had it built up here so the helmsman would have better visibility fore and aft. It's great for spotting fish or watching the trawl. Leaves a lot more room for the galley too."

"By golly!" said Catfish, "*that's* what Sorry meant when he grumbled about the Navy spreading his work all over the boat."

"That's what I *thought* he meant, Captain, but I didn't dare ask him," Kip said and laughed.

All the boys could see of the man at the helm was his back, he was so crowded in by various kinds of equip-

ment. He was a big man in a wrinkled dark blue uniform
and a battered captain's cap. Most of him blotted out the
ship's wheel and half of the instruments in front of him.

"This is Big Clyde," said Catfish, introducing the boys
to the helmsman. "He used to be in the Merchant Marine.
Knows ships forwards or backwards. Reads 'em like a
book."

The big seaman seemed reluctant to leave his wheel,
but he reached out a horny catcher's mitt of a hand and
wrung theirs. Big Clyde didn't seem to have a neck but if
he did have one the boys couldn't see it for his bushy
black beard. Nor could they see his eyes. He kept them in
a perpetual squint. Shandy could tell he was deeply
engrossed in keeping the *Elmira* on course so it was best
not to bother him. Besides, there were more interesting
things to see in the pilothouse. Much of it was electronic
gear unfamiliar to the boys—gray metal boxes with many
black knobs and glass dials, some with antennas and some
without. One that looked like an expensive portable radio
had a round metal hoop on top as thick as the handle of a
baseball bat and almost as big as a steering wheel. The
only thing either of them recognized was the fathometer
mounted to the right of the helm. It was similar to the one
on Catfish's houseboat and they knew that when it was
switched on it would record the water depth by drawing a
contour line of the bottom on a slowly moving drum of
paper.

The captain briefed them on the trawler's standard
equipment—the radiotelephone he called a "squawk box"
for talking to other boats or stations on shore; the automatic pilot which if needed would keep the trawler on
course even with no one tending the wheel; the radio
direction finder for taking bearings on radio stations, then

plotting their directions on a chart to locate the correct position of the boat; and a long-range radio navigation instrument called a loran for obtaining extremely accurate position fixes up to 1400 miles at sea.

When Catfish finished, Kip explained his equipment for locating sensors. "Actually what we have is pretty experimental right now," he told them. "We don't know whether it will work or not. We do know, however, that the sensors are transmitting a signal on a certain frequency and that's what we have this special receiver tuned for." He touched an instrument that looked like an ordinary marine radio. "It works something like our RDF system—"

"RDF?" said Jib.

"Sorry, Jib—the radio direction finder."

"Yes, sir."

"The main difference," Kip continued, "is that we're hunting for underwater signals. So the antenna for this unit is a probe built into the hull just under the bow. Unfortunately the receiver's range isn't much more than two thousand feet—we checked it out on the sensors we've got. That means we have to be pretty close to any shark carrying those things or we won't get a signal."

"What kind of signal is it?" asked Shandy.

"A single, short tone oscillation repeated at one-second intervals at maximum range. The faster it beeps the closer the sensor is to the boat. A continuous tone means it's directly under us."

"What if the sensors aren't all the same frequency?" asked Shandy.

"We had that possibility in mind when we installed this item." Kip tapped a rectangular box with two knobs and a needle gauge on its front and a single knob on its side. "It's called a radio-frequency indicator and it's also hooked up to our underwater antenna. All you have to do is twist the dials and the needle will tell you if there is a sensor around and on what frequency it is operating."

"Goll-y!" exclaimed Jib. "With all these things we shouldn't have any trouble tracking down those sharks."

"The real trick will be to catch the right shark after we find him," said Kip. "And I'm afraid that's your problem, Captain."

Catfish nodded. "All I can tell you is, we'll do our best."

"I know you will," Kip said with a smile. "Got any suggestions where we should start?"

"Well, I figure it'll take us about four hours or better to get out to the hundred-fathom curve. So why don't we save the longlines until tomorrow and fish closer in today?"

"Sounds okay to me."

"What are longlines, Catfish?"

"Just what the word says, Jib—a half-mile-long or longer length of quarter-inch Manila rope with baited hooks dangling from it on branch lines. It's a commercial fishing rig the Japanese thought up. You can sink it or float it. The way we use it for sharks is to float it with oil drums on each end."

"Then we can catch a lot of sharks at one time?"

"Right. When they get on, all you have to do is winch them in and rebait. Chances are we'll put out some trot-lines first—they're short longlines. Scatter a few sets around the area, then wait for the sharks to come to us. If things look good, then we'll string out our longlines and really go to town."

"How about this spot you mentioned that was closer in, Captain?"

"It's a place we call Shark Alley, Kip. An old tanker that

was sunk during the war. We can fish it with regular tackle and dynamite."

"Fish with dynamite!" exclaimed Shandy.

"Right," said Catfish. "You can fill the boys in on the details while you're getting rigged up, Kip. I'll put Clyde on the new course."

"Fine, skipper."

Clear for Action

When Kip headed for the shrimp hold the boys were right on his heels. With the anticipation of what was coming, Jib had even forgotten about being seasick.

"What did he mean about dynamite?" Shandy asked as they went down the aft ladder into the large cabin where the fishing tackle was stowed.

"Well, an underwater explosion is one of the quickest ways to attract sharks." Kip pulled a big tackle box out from under one of the berths and opened it. "You see, sound travels a tremendous distance underwater and sharks have a sense of hearing that scientists believe may be even keener than their sense of smell. They can detect and follow a scent as dilute as one part of blood to fifty million parts of water, which is practically no scent at all. A shark uses his nose as a homing device: when a scent comes stronger in one nostril, he turns in that direction. But his sense of hearing is so good that he can detect the feeble vibrations of a swimming fish when he is so far away that he can neither see nor smell it."

"I never even knew that sharks had ears," said Jib.

Kip smiled. "They don't—at least not the way other animals do. A shark hears by an organ we call a lateral line, a network of nerve tunnels which run the length of his body and fan out on his head and jaw. Reaching up

54

vertically from the tunnels are shafts that end as large pores of the skin. These are the shark's ears, but you might say he listens with his whole body. What he hears and translates into meaning are low-frequency sound waves traveling through the water at five thousand feet a second. When he picks up the sound waves of an under-water explosion, he can't resist coming to see what's happened."

"I don't understand that," said Shandy. "If I were a shark it'd scare me off."

Kip found the 12/0 Soby hooks he was looking for in his tackle box and checked their barbs.

"Not if you were a shark," he told Shandy. "Figure it out for yourself. If there's an explosion it means only one thing to a shark—food. Something edible is certain to have been stunned or killed by the blast and he won't take long coming to find out what it was."

"Gosh, just like a dinner bell!" Jib exclaimed. "How do you suppose they figured that out?"

"We taught them," said Kip, touching up the barbs of some of his hooks with a file.

"We did?" the boys asked in surprise.

"Mankind did, without knowing it," said Kip. "Under-water explosions in nature are rare—in fact, they probably never occur except in cases of a volcanic upheaval somewhere in the bottom of the ocean. All other explosions are man-made. An airplane crashes into the sea and explodes; a ship is torpedoed during a war; a bomb is dropped on some atoll. All of these things have condi-tioned sharks, have taught them to expect food when they hear an explosion. World War II was probably one of the best shark-conditioning environments man could have de-vised."

"Gosh, I guess so." Shandy shuddered at the thought.

"Anyway," said Kip, "you'll see how we use the dynamite when we get to the wreck. Now how about helping me lug the rods and tackle topside?"

"You bet!" the boys answered in unison and headed for the row of big rods and reels hanging in cradle supports from the overhead deck beams.

An hour later Catfish took a final loran reading and gave orders to drop anchor. The *Elmira* settled back against her chain, her bow pointed southwest into the prevailing breeze. With characteristic ease she adopted the rhythm of the calming sea, riding the ground swell with just enough of a roll to sway the midship booms and creak the standing rigging.

As far as the eye could see, the Gulf was a royal-blue carpet rippling with a perfect pattern of wavelets mirroring millions of eye-tingling suns. Overhead a less glaring but equally blue sky became a backdrop for dozens of white-winged sea gulls that had instinctively recognized the vessel as a shrimp boat. Down they swooped with shrill cries, investigating the trawler's gurgling wake in high hopes of finding the usual free lunch. When none was forthcoming, they rose and swept up abeam the boat, canting their slender white wings and hovering in midair while scolding the seamen as only sea gulls can.

Catfish stuck his head out the wheelhouse window and hailed the boys on the fantail. "Put out your rigs! This is Shark Alley!"

"Aye aye, skipper!" Shandy waved.

The whole crew came aft to lend a hand.

Kip and the boys had already spaced the big rods and reels along the gunwales and rigged the end tackle for each. The reels were the finest Shandy and Jib had ever seen—huge solid-brass Swedish *Fin-Nors* that purred like kittens when their handles were turned. Two were 9/o's, the same size as the one Shandy had used to catch the tiger shark. The other two were 12/0's, each as large as a volleyball. All the line was Dacron—eighty-pound-test on the smaller reels, 130-pound-test on the larger. This was big-game fishing equipment, the kind, Kip explained, that was most often used to catch the greatest fighting fish of all—marlin, the rapier-billed species that could fight for seven and eight hours and could weigh more than half a ton.

"Not all sharks are in the same fighting class as marlin," Kip told the boys as they tied each line to thirty feet of plastic-covered tiller cable leader. "Some are bigger, but only one species of shark, the mako, can fight as fiercely as the finest black marlin, which big-game fishermen consider the champion of them all."

"But how does a mako fight that's different from the way other sharks fight?" asked Shandy as they baited the big hooks with half-frozen three-pound bonitos from Sorry's deep freeze.

"Most sharks are powerhouse fighters," Kip explained. "They stay deep and pour on the steam—at least twenty out of some three hundred members in the family do. The rest are sluggish or small fish not worth the angler's bother. The blacktips and spinner sharks are spectacular fighters because they leap like tarpon. The tigers and great whites are sought after because of their size and fierceness. But the mako is something else. He grows over twelve feet long and weighs more than a thousand pounds. When he grabs your bait and runs, it's like being tied to a thunderbolt. He'll strip off a hundred yards of line in a flash, then explode out of water like a Polaris missile, hurling his body ten to fifteen feet in the air, whirling as he goes, trying to wrap line and leader around himself to break it."

"Wow!" breathed Shandy.

"And that's only the beginning," said Kip. "As soon as he crashes back into the sea, he spins out again. He can keep that up for hours as long as you have him on . . . or as long as he has *you* on," the oceanographer said with a chuckle.

"Boy, would I like to hang into one of those makos today!" said Shandy.

"Whoa, wait a minute! Don't wish that on us," said Kip. "We'd be with that fish all day long. Just find us another tiger with one of those yellow balls in his stomach and you'll have your day's work done."

"We'll try, won't we, Jib?"

"You bet!"

Catfish came aft with his swordfish cap tilted low over his eyes to shield them against the glare.

"How's it coming?"

"About to get organized, Captain. What do you think would be the best bet—fish the top or bottom?"

"They're liable to be either place, Kip. The wreck's off our starboard stern about fifty yards. Got a good picture of it on the fathometer when we came over. She's in forty-five fathoms. Why don't you put a couple of baits on top and a couple on the bottom? That should cover it."

"Good idea."

"What about the dynamite?"

"It's locked in the safe. I'll bring it up as soon as we launch the rigs." Kip looked around. Rooster and Sorry were screwing a meat grinder to a plank and getting ready to set up a chum line. The Greek was separating frozen fish so they would fit into the maw of the grinder. "Where's Big Clyde?"

"I left him in the wheelhouse so he could keep his ear cocked for anything that might come over your radio."

Kip nodded as he tied twelve-ounce bell leads on the

brass line-to-leader swivels of the two largest shark rigs. "On the second shelf of the tackle box you'll find a paper sack with balloons in it," he told the boys. "Blow up a couple and tie one to each of the swivels on the rigs we'll float. That'll let those baits hang thirty feet down while the other two are on bottom at two hundred and seventy feet."

The boys found the balloons and were blowing them up when Kip said, "If you've got any air left, blow up a third balloon. I've got an idea."

Catfish checked the drags on all the reels to make sure they were adjusted properly. The *Fin-Nors* had a lever on the right-reel plate for that purpose. When the lever was moved forward or backward, line could be pulled out under varying degrees of pressure without the reel handle's turning. If the drag was set too loose, the line would slip when the angler struck his fish and there would be insufficient force to set the hook. If it was too tight, the fish might break the line on his first rush.

Sorry and Rooster finally got the meat grinder going. The cook had lugged a carton of canned chicken noodle soup out of the galley and was using it as a support to hold the meat grinder off the deck while he sat on the board and box and cranked the handle. Rooster fed in the baitfish while Jonah caught the ground-up results in a small plastic bucket. As soon as the bucket was full he tossed handfuls over the side into the water. The current scattered the particles into the depths like falling snow-flakes.

"As soon as Mr. Shark gets a whiff of this Greek's fine chum line he be following it up fast for bigger handout."

"We'll be ready" said Jib as they finished tying the balloons to the lines.

"Better not put out too much chum at a time," Catfish

cautioned Jonah. "All we want to do is whet those sharks' appetites—not satisfy it."

Kip stripped off some line from one of the reels, coiled the long leader in his right hand, and began swinging the bait.

"Here's something they can satisfy themselves on," he said and heaved the leader, line, and bait combination over the side.

The balloon immediately acted as a bobber and sail. It kept the heavy bait from sinking while the breeze slowly pushed the balloon downwind, taking out more line as it went.

Jib and Shandy launched their baits the same way from the other side of the cockpit. The rods were then propped against the gunwales, leaning well back so only a foot of their tips protruded over the rail. This was done to prevent the sudden strike of a shark from catapulting the rod and reel over the side before someone could get to it.

Kip dropped the fourth baited line straight to the bottom beneath the trawler.

"Keep your eyes on the balloons and don't let out more than fifty yards of line," Kip told the boys. "Catfish and I will get the dynamite."

By the time they came back, Shandy had snapped on the reels' clickers and stopped the outgoing lines at what he judged was the right distance.

Catfish was carrying a large spool of yellow cable wire while Kip had some brown paper packages and a six-volt dry-cell battery under his arm.

"We're going to need a bunch of balloons to tie on the cable as we let it out," he said with a meaningful glance at the boys. "How're your lungs holding out?"

"Great," Shandy laughed. "How many balloons do you want?"

"A dozen should do it. We'll tie them on as we let it out."

With much huffing and puffing the boys started on the balloons. Kip rigged up three sticks of dynamite to detonators, then wired them to one end of the cable and wrapped the whole package with waxed paper and plastic electrical tape. Heavy lead weights were attached and the combination was carefully held over the side and lowered almost to the bottom. Then the balloons were tied on, one after another, six feet apart as more cable went out and the balloons carried it astern until it was strung out for a considerable distance behind the trawler.

Then, with utmost care, Kip attached one of the wires of the cable to a battery terminal. The tip of the other wire was shielded with tape until he removed it and held the wire well away from the battery.

"Is everybody ready?" he called.

"Yes sir."

"Go ahead—touch it off."

Kip moved the wire to the bare terminal.

The explosion sounded like distant thunder. The boys felt the concussion through their feet and that was all. They were both disappointed. Here they were expecting a big bang and a towering geyser, and all they got was a hollow thud they'd almost have missed if they hadn't been listening closely. Seconds later the surface of the sea boiled once and turned the color of gray mud. Then the sea gulls appeared again from nowhere to swoop diving and squawking into the disturbed water, rising as soon as they touched, clutching stunned or dead fish in their beaks. With two or three rapid gulps they downed their catch and zoomed back into the fray.

"At least we made a big hit with the sea gulls," Catfish observed.

"Let's hope we make just as big a hit with the sharks," said Shandy.

"We will," promised Kip. He picked up the heavy rod on which he had ballooned out their third bait.

"What are you going to do?" asked Jib.

"I cut off the lip of the balloon so I could drop the bait right over the wreck."

"But what's the lip of the balloon got to do with it?"

"Watch." Kip flipped his reel into gear, reeled up slack line, then suddenly struck the rod violently, heaving it back as hard as he could. The abrupt movement jerked the balloon free of the line. The lead weight carried the bait to the bottom beside the wreck.

"Gosh, that was neat!" cried Jib.

"That's about the only way you can do it with tackle this heavy, Jib. You can't cast it so you take advantage of things like winds and currents and tides to put your bait where you want it."

"Sometimes they even use kites," said Catfish, "and a friend of mine down in Lake Worth launches his shark bait with candy."

"Kites!" exclaimed Jib.

"Candy?" asked Shandy. They both frowned.

"Sure. The kite is tied to a separate reel of line. All you have to do is clip your leader to a clothespin on the kite, fly it to where you want to drop your bait, then jerk your fishing line out of the clothespin. It works great. In some places they even use kites to skip baits to catch sailfish and marlin."

"Kites maybe . . . but *candy?*" pursued Shandy.

Catfish grinned. "Yep, even candy. A roll of Life Savers with a hole through the middle. Herb Goodman came up with the idea a couple years ago. Herb's a one-man shark club down in south Florida. He never uses a boat so he has to fight his sharks from the beach—big brutes, too—some of them twelve-foot hammerheads. Herb's problem was how to get his baits—usually two six-pound bonitos with a couple of sash weights in their stomachs—into deep water offshore. That's when he came up with the idea of using candy. He calls it his 'weak link.' He ties two balloons to a loop of line that passes through the roll of Life Savers and back to the balloons. Another loop threads through the same hole in the candy and ties to his leader-line swivel. Then he drops his rig in a runout of an outgoing tide and lets the balloons float out his baits. Herb knows exactly how long it will take the water to melt his link of candy. When it does the balloons float free and the sash weights drop the baits to the bottom three hundred yards from shore where the big sharks are."

"Why, that's pure genius!" marveled Shandy.

"You're right," agreed Catfish. "But then Herb's a mighty devoted shark fisherman. If you want to do a thing badly enough, no matter how impossible it seems, there's usually a way to do it. All it takes is some thought."

Suddenly there was a yell from the pilothouse.

"What's up?" called Catfish.

Big Clyde's excited reply made their hair stand on end.

"Tell Kip his radio rig here is beeping up a storm!"

Shark Alley

The words were hardly out of Big Clyde's mouth when the clicker on one of the 12/0's stuttered shrilly, then stopped.

The men froze. Every eye was on the big reel. They waited, still, tense, hardly breathing. . . .

"Maybe he's only—"

"*R-r-r-r-rp! . . . R-r-r-r-rp! . . . R-r-r-r-rrrrrrrrrreeeeeeee!*"

"He's got it!" yelled Kip. "Take him, Shandy!"

"Get the harness and butt strap on him!"

"Where are they?"

"Behind the tackle box—"

"Don't strike him too soon."

"Hush up—kid knows what he's doing!"

Shandy gritted his teeth and struggled with the heavy rod, keeping his hands away from the blur that was the spool spinning line through the guides at top speed. The clicker rapidly jumped octaves until it was shrilling a metallic scream.

Eager hands helped him into the leather shoulder harness; others buckled the belt around his hips that would support the rod butt.

"Man, is that shark traveling!"

Shandy gripped the cork hand rest ahead of the reel, his arms straight, legs bent, leaning back slightly in his harness. He forced himself to count slowly to ten, then he said:

"Think he's had it long enough?" His voice was tight, anxious.

"Sure he has," someone said.

"Better wait," someone else cautioned. "They can carry a bait a long way in their teeth without taking it back into their mouths."

"Yeah, but this one means business—look how hard he hit. Bet he gulped it the first bite."

Beads of sweat rolled down Shandy's cheeks. "I think he's got it now, don't you?"

"I'm sure he has," said Kip.

"Go ahead, throw it to him," said Catfish.

"Okay—here goes. . . ." Shandy leaned forward slightly, then flipped the brake lever, locking the spool in gear. It took three swift seconds for the line to twang taut. At the instant it did, Shandy hauled back on the rod, throwing every ounce of strength into it—and at the same moment he felt the strength of the shark, the heavy, ponderous, driving weight that snapped him upright involuntarily and almost jerked him off his feet.

"Throw it to him again! Drive in that hook!"

Again Shandy bent forward and then tugged backward, pulling hard against the straining rod.

The shark suddenly spurted ahead.

"Look out!"

Shandy was catapulted across the deck and slammed so hard against the transom that his teeth rattled. For an instant he was pinned there like a moth against a windshield. Then they grabbed him and hauled him back. He shook his head and gulped air. The reel brake was

screeching; the spool whirred away line as if nothing were holding it, as if it were on free spool instead of having close to a hundred pounds of geared pressure restraining it.

The shark continued in a straight line away from them.

"Better turn him," someone said.

"Don'tcha think he would if he could?"

"Is that drag okay? He's sure taking line mighty fast."

Shandy reached over to check it. His palm touched the brake housing and he yelped.

"It's hot!"

"Get some water, quick!"

Sorry jogged to the galley. Seconds later he was back with a sloshing kettleful of water.

"Gangway! Look out!" The crew parted. The cook drew back and fired.

At that range he couldn't miss. He drenched the reel, Shandy, Catfish, and Kip and was drawing back for a second shot when Catfish bellowed:

"Hold it! Just wet the reel, Sorry, don't drown it and us too!"

"Sorry 'bout that, Cap'n."

Jonah glanced at the dwindling spool of line on Shandy's reel. He shook his head.

"That's a Yankee shark sure," he muttered. "Won't turn till he gets to Miami."

But the Greek was wrong. Catfish was one breath away from ordering up the anchor and giving chase when Shandy's line suddenly went slack.

"He musta cut it!"

"Naw, that's a tiger trick. He's doubling back."

Shandy reeled furiously, picking up slack line.

"Can you feel anything?" asked Jib.

"Uh-uh . . . nothing."

"You suppose he did cut it?"

"How could he with a leader that long, for crying out loud!"

"Maybe this one big shark like Kerosene Joe."

"That was no shark—it was a whale."

"You bonnethead—it was a whale *shark!*"

"Okay, okay, you guys, stow it," said Catfish. "What do you think, Shandy. Did he cut it?"

"I don't know . . . the shark I caught the other night did the same thing."

"They can fool you," said Kip.

Abruptly the line snapped taut and there was no doubt

about it now. The Dacron slashed the water on an oblique angle across the stern.

"Hey—he's still on!" Shandy yelled happily.

"See! What'd I tell ya?" crowed Rooster.

"R-r-r-rprrrrrrreeeeeeeee!" squalled another reel.

Catfish leaped as if he'd been stung. "Oh my gosh! We forgot to bring in the other rigs! Did he cross the line?"

Kip had already snatched up the rod and snapped off the clicker, at the same time using his thumb as the lightest of brakes against the rapidly revolving spool. He looked to see where Shandy's line was.

"I think it's another shark," he said.

Catfish and Jonah wasted no time reeling in the remaining lines, something that should have been done the minute the first shark was hooked to prevent fouling.

Kip waited until they were out of his way, then he threw the reel on brake and struck the rod hard, jerking it back swiftly three times to set the hook solidly in the shark's jaw.

The instant bow of the rod and screech of the brake indicated he had succeeded. The line streaked in a satisfying sizzle across the surface to port.

Kip glanced around. "Here, Jib—get on this thing." He held out the lively flexing rod.

"Who, me?" Jib jumped back as if he had been offered a writhing rattlesnake.

"Sure, you." Kip grinned. "Take it—you can handle him."

"I don't know . . . I never—"

"Go ahead, Jib. We'll give you all the help you need," Catfish encouraged.

"But—what if I lose him?"

"You won't." Kip thrust the equipment into his hands.

Jib grasped the thick rod in a death grip, his eyes

practically popping out of their sockets when he felt what was happening on the other end of his line. Rooster struggled to make him release his clenched fists, one at a time, long enough to get a harness over his shoulders.

"Holy mackerel!" Jib gasped as the line zipped into a strumming "U" turn. "Holy mackerel!" he gasped again when the shark straightened his run and dragged the boy heels first toward the gunwale, bending him over it.

Bubbling with mirth, Jonah dropped a heavy hand into the gaping neck of Jib's shoulder harness and hauled him back on even keel again, that being a forty-five-degree angle to the deck—the only stance there is to counterbalance a fish with the disposition of a runaway train. And both boys were hooked to such fish.

The only difference was that Shandy's shark thought it was a long-distance express. It made long straight runs that almost depleted the line on the spool, then curved back, far out, while Shandy gained what line he could, pumping and cranking, only to lose it all again on another long dash.

Jib's shark preferred to stay deep but closer to the boat. The crew encouraged the sweat-drenched boy to keep pumping, keep reeling, keep hauling, until the shark begrudgingly let him gain some line. The shark let him think it was giving in, let him dare to hope that in a minute his aching muscles would have a chance to relax, that he could wipe the stinging sweat out of his eyes, that the end was near. But the others knew better. The shark gave only enough to spark these hopes; then it reversed its ground and ripped away with the hard-gained line. It went on like this for almost an hour, then something happened to Shandy's shark.

"He's coming in," he warned them. "I can tell—I can feel him bulldogging, but he's coming!"

Jonah fashioned a running noose in a heavy Manila line, leaving plenty of slack and tying the loose end around the winch drum.

The long taut angle between Shandy's line and the surface of the water was slowly diminishing.

There was a shout from the pilothouse. Big Clyde was pointing.

Then they all saw it. First the long dark shimmering shadow . . . then something black rose up out of the water until it towered like a thick, limber sail over the shadow.

"What a dorsal fin!"

"That's no tiger shark!" Kip exclaimed. "He's a hammerhead! Big one!"

"Big one is right! Where's the wire cutters? We can't bring that thing aboard!"

"Don't cut him off until I get a tag into him," said Kip as he headed for his cabin at a trot.

Shandy saw his shark more clearly now. It was coasting in on an angle, the long streamlined grayish body bigger than a lifeboat; the broad ugly hammer-shaped head wider than Shandy knew he could reach even with both arms outstretched. A shivery tingle ran down his spine.

"Jib, can you see him?"

"Yeah, he's a beaut!"

"How's yours coming?"

"Okay—if my back holds up. He's going around in circles down deep but I can't get him up."

"See if you can—" Shandy was abruptly jerked up on the balls of his feet as the big hammerhead saw the hull of the trawler for the first time and veered off on a swift, spiraling dive that screeched the reel brake.

"If those two sharks get together down there we're in trouble," said Catfish.

Kip came up with his tagging rifle. "What happened?"

"The hammer took a look at us and didn't like what he saw."

But Shandy was pumping his rod and gaining line again.

"He's coming this time—coming up right beside us."

Kip braced himself at the rail and brought the rifle up to his shoulder. "When he shows, keep his head up. Try to get his back out of water."

"I'll try." Shandy strained to hoist, then dipped the rod tip for a quick grab at the temporarily slack line.

The shark rolled ponderously to the surface, turning half over to show its white underside, its gaping maw of white teeth. The round buttonlike eye on its right head lobe glared menacingly up at the fishermen.

Kip's rifle snicked like an air gun. The white plastic dart stamped with an identification number stuck firmly in the shark's leathery hide just ahead of the massive dorsal fin.

"Nice shot!" cried Shandy.

Jonah grabbed the flexible cable leader with gloved hands. The huge shark swung its broad head like a battering ram, slamming the trawler's hull with vicious blows that almost knocked the Greek off his feet. Still he hung on doggedly.

"Where's those wire cutters?"

"Here—"

Catfish snatched them from Rooster and reached over the side.

Jonah's arms jerked upward as they were relieved of the straining weight. The shark paused, not realizing it was free. Then suddenly its body undulated violently and it glided off, the long caudal fin sweeping back and forth like the tail of a serpent. Two feet of leader wire trailed from the awesome jaws as the shark slowly submerged.

The last they saw of it was the tip of its tall dorsal rippling the surface. And then it was gone.

The crew immediately turned its attention to Jib, who looked as if he was in need of it. In the excitement of seeing Shandy's shark come in he had stopped fighting his own and was merely keeping pressure on his rod. But he had been leaning back in his harness for so long his hands were frozen to the rod and he was dead tired. In fact, all he had strength to do was huff and puff beads of sweat into the air as they rolled off the tip of his nose.

Still, when Catfish asked, "Want me to take him awhile, Jib, so you can catch a breather?" he answered the captain with a determined shake of his head.

"I'm going to land him if I—if I have to stay here all night to do it."

"That's the spirit." Kip smiled with approval. "Can you get any line?"

"Not much," Jib said. "He was right under the boat once, then he headed out and went deep. Since then I've had a hard time moving him."

Jib turned the 9/0's handle but the spool never budged.

"Hope he hasn't fouled the line on the wreck," said Catfish.

"Try winching him," suggested Shandy.

"What do you mean?"

"Let the harness and butt strap support your rod and use your hands to keep the spool from turning. Then walk backwards and haul with your whole body."

"Okay—I just hope I don't break the line."

"You won't."

Jib tried what Shandy suggested, bracing the spool and hauling on the rod with every step. Bent as he was he looked like an overweight drum major strutting backward in slow motion. It may have looked funny but it was no

laughing matter to the stout boy. The rod butt was jabbing a hole through his stomach, his back felt as if it were
breaking and the head of steam he had built up was
making his eardrums thunder.

But the line did come a few feet.

"Pick up what you can and try again," urged Kip.

Jib straightened up and staggered back to the gunwale,
reeling as he went. Once again he gritted his teeth,
clenched his eyes and sweated his way backward, gaining
more line. Then, without warning, the shark moved, heading north.

"Get up to the side!" shouted Catfish. "Don't let him
take your line into the rigging or he's a goner!"

Jib lunged for the gunwale. The shark kept going in the
direction of the bow.

"Now back to the stern! Lean on him all you can—turn
him!"

Jib did as he was told. He was beyond feeling now. All
that mattered was that he had to turn the shark, had to
make it swing back toward him before the shark crossed
the bow, cutting the line on the ship's hull.

From the corner of the stern he gave the rod every
ounce of strength he possessed, plus a bit more he never
knew he had. Through his numbed arms he sensed rather
than felt the faint, stubborn bulldog movements of the
shark struggling to keep from turning. But gradually it
gave . . . begrudgingly it began to swerve. And then it
finally turned.

While they cheered Jib, they advised him: "Reel! Reel
like mad!"

And reel he did, palming the sweat-slick fist-sized
plastic handle of his reel and cranking it for all he was
worth.

"He's coming up. Get that tail rope ready, Jonah!"

The shark swept darkly to the surface, its unusually broad, blunt head plowing the water ahead of its long, striped gray body.

"Good golly, it's a tiger!" shouted Catfish. "Get a snapper line on the leader, quick! Where's the shotgun?"

There was a mad rush as the crew scrambled to ready gear for boating the shark. Rooster raced to the forecastle for the captain's 12-gauge shark dispatcher; Jib reeled in line until the leader swivel was within reach. Kip leaned out with the snapper line—a 1000-pound-test nylon rope spliced to a chrome swivel clip. With one hand he clipped the snapper line to the leader swivel; with the other he cut the Dacron fishing line. Now, instead of being tethered to the rod and reel, the shark was connected to a strong, pliable nylon rope that allowed more than one man to hold him. Shandy helped Jib unharness himself from his rod and then they joined Kip and Catfish on the snapper line.

The shark rolled and thrashed, smashing down heavily with its caudal fin, showering the fishermen bent over the rail.

Catfish blinked salt water out of his eyes and squinted toward the forecastle.

"C'mon, Rooster!" he yelled.

Jonah and Sorry tried their best to lasso the shark's thrashing tail section but their loop missed its mark repeatedly.

The shark became more violent.

"Somebody better go fetch Rooster," Catfish grunted. "He must have fallen overboard."

"No—here he comes!" Shandy saw the bandy-legged little Mexican hurrying toward them with the double-barreled shotgun.

The shark began purposefully heaving its massive body

over and over in a series of rolls; each time it turned, the awesome jaws snapped like a giant bear trap on the thin but strong leader wire. Suddenly a saclike mass emerged from its mouth.

"Look out! He's spitting his stomach—he'll throw the hook for sure!"

Rooster rushed to the rail and shouldered the shotgun, aiming down.

"Shoot!"

The 12-gauge roared; a wall of water exploded in their faces.

"Give him the other barrel—"

A second blast and geyser of water cut off the captain's words.

The shark continued to lash the sea to foam but not nearly as violently now. Jonah managed to get the tail rope over the tiger's caudal fin just as the hook pulled loose from the shark's stomach. When this happened, everyone grabbed the rope Jonah and Sorry were holding. All together they slowly hoisted the tiger tail first up the side of the boat, over the rail and onto the deck. With profound relief, Shandy and Jib shook hands.

"Whew!" gasped Kip. "No wonder you had trouble bringing him in, Jib. This tiger's no amateur; he knew a few tricks."

Sorry paced off the length of the shark at a cautious distance.

"Nine and a half feet long," he reported.

Jib stared at his awesome catch, hardly able to believe that he had fought and landed it—a fish that weighed probably three times as much as he did. He wiped his forehead and glanced at Kip.

"Did he do that on purpose—throwing out his stomach like that?"

"You bet he did," said Kip. "Sharks can evert their stomachs, bring them up and turn them inside out, as easily as you could turn your pocket inside out."

"Just so he could twist free of the hook?" asked Shandy.

"That's right," Kip nodded. "Had the hook lodged in his jaw he wouldn't have done that."

"But if it had worked—if he had gotten free—would he have swallowed his stomach again?"

"Sure. Same way you'd push your pocket back in."

"Boy—that's weird!" murmured Jib.

"Well, one thing we can be glad about," said Catfish, "the hook came loose before he coughed up the whole works. Maybe we're in luck."

"In luck?" With the excitement of catching the sharks, Jib had forgotten about what they were after. "Oh yeah—" he said, remembering. "Do you think maybe—?"

Catfish reached for his knife. "We'll know in a minute."

Rooster and Sorry rolled the shark's carcass over. Catfish made the incision like a practiced surgeon. For a moment he groped up to his elbows inside the fish. Suddenly his face lighted up. He withdrew his arms.

In his hands was a glistening yellow sensor!

Shandy's pulse quickened. Catching the first tiger shark from the beach and finding the strange object in its stomach had been an accident. But zeroing in on this one far from shore was no accident. How many more man-eaters were carrying the mysterious yellow balls. And where would the next one lead them? To the source—the answer to the mystery itself?

Shandy glanced up suddenly and swept his eyes slowly across the vacant horizon. He did not have the slightest idea what he was looking for but he had the strangest feeling that at that very moment someone was watching them.

A Four-Hundred-Million-Year-Old Computer?

When the excitement of catching the two sharks and finding the sensor simmered down, Sorry headed for the galley to fix dinner while the others rebaited and put out the shark rigs again. Then Jonah relieved Big Clyde in the wheelhouse, Rooster disappeared down the engine-room hatch, Catfish retreated into the shade of the deckhouse for a nap, and Kip set to work cutting out the jaws of the tiger shark as a trophy for the boys. It was a slow, tedious job because the shark's hide was so tough Kip repeatedly had to stop to resharpen his knife. As they watched him, Shandy and Jib questioned him about their catch.

"I'll bet sharks have the toughest skin in the world, haven't they?" Jib asked when he saw the trouble Kip was having to cut it.

"I don't know about that but it can certainly dull the sharpest knife in the world," said Kip.

"That's what's always seemed funny to me," said Shandy. I read once that a shark's hide was so rough that if it brushed against you it would scrape off skin."

Kip nodded. "Like sandpaper."

"But it's only rough in one direction." Shandy slid his hand along the flank of the dead tiger shark. "When you rub toward the tail it feels . . . well, not smooth but still your hand slides. But if you try to slide your hand in the other direction—toward his head—it sticks right there. It's rougher than a cat's tongue. Why's that?"

Kip thought about it for a while so he could explain it in a way the boys would understand.

"You've heard the expression 'he's armed to the teeth,' haven't you?"

"Yes."

"Well, a shark is literally armed to the teeth *with* teeth. He has them from head to tail. If you were to put a piece of shark skin under a microscope you'd see what I mean. The surface of his skin is covered with billions of tiny, sharp microscopic teeth called denticles. Most fish have scales but these dermal denticles of the shark are true teeth—each one is covered by dentine like our teeth and each contains a nerve and blood vessels the same way as ours. The reason your hand slides when you move it toward his tail and sticks when you try to push it toward his head, Shandy, is that the shark's skin teeth all slant backward."

"I wonder what for?"

"Probably to help the shark swim; perhaps even to feel with or to hear—like microscopic antennas."

Jib touched the shark's coarse hide to feel it for himself. "Gee, that's almost as weird as being able to turn his stomach inside out whenever he wants to," he commented.

"Ohhh, I don't know," said Kip, holding up the shark's enormous jaws and examining them critically. "For a fish that doesn't have a bone in his body, never seems to sleep, and has to swim constantly, the trick with his stomach isn't too strange."

"No bone in his body?" The boys stared at their friend skeptically.

"That's right," said Kip. "Sharks don't have bones—their skeletons are cartilage. It's a flexible substance like gristle. When I cut out these jaws I had to be careful because it was hard to tell when I was cutting meat and when I was cutting the cartilage, it's that much alike. Of course once the jaws dry for a few days the cartilage will get almost as hard as bone."

"What about their never having to sleep and swimming all the time?" Shandy asked.

"I said they never *seem* to sleep—and chances are it's not sleep as we know it. You see fish have swim bladders that enable them to remain almost motionless at any depth of water they choose. The swim bladder is like a small balloon of air located just under the backbone and above the intestines. A fish can either inflate it to a point of neutral buoyancy so he will neither rise to the top nor sink to the bottom; or he can inflate it or deflate it to go up or down. A shark doesn't have an air bladder, so he lacks any kind of flotation device. The specific gravity of his body is such that if he stops swimming, he immediately sinks to the bottom."

"That might not be so bad," said Jib. "Maybe then he could rest and get some sleep."

"You may be right," said Kip, "if he happens to be a shark that comes into shallow water. But if he's a true pelagic or ocean-going shark like a mako or a blue and he stops to take a snooze in mid-ocean, he will drop a mile or more beneath the surface in less than an hour. No," said Kip, "if a shark sleeps at all, chances are he only dozes for brief periods, but in the main he must keep swimming from the day he is born until the day he dies."

Jib couldn't imagine anything worse unless it was being hungry all the time. Catfish had told them once that sharks were always hungry.

"I guess I wouldn't care much about being a shark," Jib admitted, realizing that he was already beginning to feel the pangs of a somewhat sharklike appetite.

Shandy leaned forward as Kip laboriously cut a layer of skin out of the inside of the jaws.

"Wow! Look at all those teeth! They're as big as arrowheads!"

"And razor-sharp," said Kip. He spread the jaws so the boys could see inside them easily. "Notice how the first row stands straight up and the other four rows lie back flat, overlapping each other."

"Yeahhhh." The boys carefully touched several of the jagged white points. "Boy, wouldn't he be in a fix if he got a toothache?" said Shandy.

"Not as bad a fix as you'd think," said Kip. "Mother Nature makes it pretty easy for a shark. If he loses or breaks off one of his front teeth, the next one in line simply moves up and takes its place. A shark never runs out of teeth because he's always got a replacement."

"I wish Mother Nature took care of my teeth like that," said Jib. "I'd never have to go to a dentist."

"How many teeth do you suppose he's got—counting those that are folded back and all?" asked Shandy.

"It's easy enough to figure," said Kip. He counted the shark's front row of teeth. "This one's got forty-two all the way around his jaw. Multiply that by five rows and he has . . . two hundred and ten in all."

"Gosh!" exclaimed the boys.

"Some have as many as a thousand," Kip added. "And this shark's great ancestor—a ninety-footer from prehistoric times—had teeth the size of your hand."

Jib scratched his head. "How'd you ever learn so much about sharks and fish and things like that?" he asked.

Kip laughed. "From reading, Jib. When you study to be

an oceanographer or a marine biologist or an ichthyologist, you learn a lot about the sea and the things in it. Even after you graduate you never stop reading and learning and remembering and seeing things for yourself." Kip paused and smiled. "I guess once you've got the bug to learn about things like this, you never get it out of your system."

A look of disappointment crossed Jib's face. "Gee whiz," he said, "I don't think I could even learn to pronounce the names of what it was you said you study to be—let alone understand about all the rest."

Kip winked at Shandy. "Someday you will, Jib. You wait and see." Shandy felt secretly flattered by the significance of the wink—that he and Kip *did* understand about those things.

"How do you mount shark jaws after they're all cleaned up?" Shandy asked.

"Just prop them open with two sticks—one up and down and the other crossways of the jaws—then lay them out in the sun to dry," said Kip. "In a few days when they turn hard you can take out the sticks and shellac the jaws, then they'll be ready to hang on your wall."

"They'll sure make a swell trophy, won't they, Jib?"

"You bet. You know something else? I bet we could scare the daylights out of your Aunt Tilou with them." Jib giggled at the thought.

"Ummmm," said Shandy reflectively. "Trouble is, she'd probably bust her broom over our heads for trying it too."

With that sobering thought, Jib lost interest in the idea.

Shandy quickly went back to the subject at hand. "Why do you have to use two sticks to prop open the jaws instead of one?" he asked Kip.

"For one reason, they warp easily. That's because a shark's jaws are hinged in four places instead of two like ours." He held them up for them to see.

"All I see is two," said Jib.

"Better look again then, Jib, because this tiger of yours not only could open and close his jaws up and down, but he could close them from side to side so he could get every tooth in his mouth into his meals, thanks to these hinges in the middle of his upper and lower jaws." Kip flexed the jaws to show the boys what he meant. The joints were so limber that he could fold the whole set into a compact V.

Shandy shook his head in wonder. "Boy, I never knew there was so much to learn about sharks," he said. "I always thought they were just nuisances—about the simplest, dumbest fish in the sea. But they're really not so dumb after all . . . and the way they're made sure isn't very simple."

"I'll have to go along with that," Kip said. "Old Mother Nature does a pretty good job providing for her own—even for her nuisances." He glanced thoughtfully at the tiger. "Just looking at him, you'd never guess that a shark is one of the oldest specialized computers in existence, would you?"

The boys frowned. "A computer?"

"One of the best, said Kip. "In fact, the first model for this one was so good that Mother Nature hasn't had to change the design for four hundred million years. She made him right the first time."

"But what does he compute?"

"The most important thing there is to a shark—how to get food. Everything about him, from his teeth to his tail, is designed for that single purpose. What little brain he has is programed with just one all-compelling equation—Life equals Food. And that's an equation a shark is well equipped to handle."

Jib sighed and stood up to stretch his legs. He looked uneasy. When Shandy asked him if he felt all right, he complained that his stomach was rumbling. Fortunately, however, the cure was close at hand.

"I really hate to leave," he told them, "but all this talk is making me terribly lunchy. I think I better go see if I can give Sorry a hand." And with that, Jib turned on his heel and made a determined beeline for the galley.

Shandy watched his friend's retreat with a mixture of wonder and slight disappointment. Then he glanced apologetically at Kip.

"I guess sharks aren't the only things around that know that all-compelling equation about food," he murmured.

"Or are so well equipped to handle it," Kip said with such studied seriousness they both broke out laughing.

Since Jib had more important matters on his mind he missed hearing the muffled merriment from the stern as the galley door swung shut behind him.

"Hi, Sorry!" he said cheerfully. "What's cooking?"

The cook, stripped to his waist, glanced up glumly from a steaming kettle. "Puppy dog tails," he muttered, "and they're not done yet."

"Great!" Jib smiled and strolled over to the gas stove. Sorry continued stirring the kettle with a wooden spoon. His face was grim and the corners of his mouth turned down as if he had been sucking a lemon.

"I just dropped by to see if I could help." Jib glanced at the bubbling concoction and snatched a quick sniff between stirs.

"Succotash!" he said triumphantly.

Sorry stopped stirring and cut his eyes suspiciously at Jib.

"How old are you?"

Jib drew himself up as tall as possible. "Almost twelve," he said.

"What do you know about cooking?"

"Well . . . I know how to."

"You know how to cook?" Sorry sized him up with a doubtful squint. "Like what?"

"Well . . . things like succotash, fried·chicken, roast oysters, homemade ice cream, Catfish chowder—things like that."

"Yeah?" Sorry went back to stirring his kettle. "Tell me how you make catfish chowder."

"You mean big 'C' Catfish chowder or little 'c' catfish chowder?"

Sorry stopped stirring. "What the devil you talking about?" he said scowling, "Big sea, little sea?"

Jib drew a deep breath. "Well, there's Catfish Jackson chowder with a big 'C,' then there's just plain ol' catfish chowder with a little 'c.' There's a difference, you know."

"There is?"

"Sure. With little 'c' chowder you start off frying bacon crisp and crumbly, then you chop up a bunch of onions and fry them until they aren't crisp, then you cut up potatoes and add tomato catsup and hot sauce and boil some catfish and put it all together in an iron pot and—"

"If that's little 'c' chowder, what's big 'C' chowder?" Sorry asked curiously.

Jib grinned. "It's like succotash only better. You start the same way with the bacon and all but then you throw in everything else you can get your hands on—potatoes, carrots, corn, celery, beans, peas, okra, plenty of hot stuff and whatever fish, shrimp, oysters, or crabs you've got handy. Cook it all up and *that's* big 'C' chowder." Jib smacked his lips. "Boy, is it scrumptious. Catfish showed us how to make it—that's why it's named after him."

"Hmmmm." Sorry looked back at his kettle. He drummed the spoon on the rim thoughtfully. "Don't sound half bad," he said. "At least . . . not as bad as succotash."

He turned back to Jib and this time his habitually sour outlook was somewhat sweetened by the faint traces of a smile. It was evident that Sorry had made up his mind about something. "How'd you like to cook up a big batch of that big 'C' chowder for us right now?"

Jib's eyes widened. "You mean it?"

"Sure I mean it. You can be the boss chef of the whole works. I'll just lend a hand whenever you need it."

"Boy, that'd be swell," said Jib. "Do we have any bacon?"

"Plenty of it in the icebox."

"What about some kind of fish?"

Sorry stroked his chin thoughtfully. "Nothing in the freezer except fish bait and meat."

Jib's face fell. "We just *got* to have some kind of fish."

Sorry snapped his fingers. "I got it! Why don't we use a piece of your tiger shark?"

"Huh?"

"Sure, boy. If you never ate shark, you got a treat coming. It tastes like swordfish."

"I never ate that either," said Jib.

"Well . . . in a way it's sorta like chicken. Like the white meat of chicken."

Jib looked closely at the cook. "You kidding me?" he asked.

"Cross my heart and hope to choke on a fish bone if it ain't the truth," Sorry swore solemnly.

As far as Jib was concerned, that settled it.

"Okay, we'll use shark meat. You go out and cut off a piece and I'll get the bacon started."

"Right." Sorry pulled open a drawer and rummaged around for a couple of sharp knives. As he started for the door, Jib called to him.

"Maybe you'd better not tell the others what you want

the shark meat for—Shandy especially. He always makes believe he isn't too crazy about my cooking—you know what I mean?"

Sorry nodded vigorously. "Been up against his kind all my life, partner. Some people just got no feeling for fine cooking." Sorry winked. "If anybody asks, I'll just tell them I'm cutting off a chunk for the chum line."

And Jib was too immersed in the problems of converting Sorry's succotash into tiger chowder, Catfish style, to notice the look of glee on the cook's face as he went out the door.

Beyond the Deepwater Curve

To say that Jib's venture into making Catfish chowder using tiger shark was a success would be an understatement.

The crew clamored for double and triple helpings of the wondrous stew, praising Sorry's prowess as a cook between mouthfuls. And Sorry, following Jib's strict instructions, merely grinned like a porpoise and let the praise rain down on him until they were through eating. Or almost through—Shandy was discreetly going back for his fourth bowlful when Sorry rapped his coffee mug and stood up to make an announcement.

"Now that you've all filled your bellies and had your say about how good the chowder was, I reckon it's time we give credit where credit's due." Sorry put his hand on Jib's shoulder. "My friend Jib here is really the one who cooked up this fine concoction for you. He made it from my succotash and his tiger shark plus a few other odds and ends. So all those fine words you said don't go to me but to him. He did it all." Jib dropped his eyes modestly.

"Well I'll be frazzled!" said Catfish. "Finest chowder I ever put in my mouth. Might've known Jib had a hand in it."

To a man the crew echoed the captain's sentiments—
well, almost to a man. Shandy was strangely silent. He
looked as if he might be holding his breath but he was
only staring at his chowder bowl.

"Hey! What's wrong with Shandy? His face is purple!"

"Musta swallowed a fish bone." Big Clyde reached over
and whumped him on the back.

The blow almost knocked Shandy under the table but
at least snapped him out of his trance. He swallowed
rapidly.

"D-did . . . you . . . say . . . Jib cooked this?" he
asked hesitantly.

"Yep. All I made was the succotash he used. But he did
all the rest—the bacon, potatoes, onions, shark—"

"*Shark?*" Shandy had hoped he hadn't heard right the
first time.

"Sure, shark. His tiger shark. How'd you like it?"

Shandy swallowed again with some difficulty but his
normal color was gradually seeping back into his face.

"It tasted . . . okay at first." He looked down at his
fourth bowlful. "Right now I wish you hadn't told me,
though."

Everyone but Shandy thought that was the funniest
thing they had ever heard. At least that's the way it
sounded to Shandy, who thought they never would stop
laughing. They asked him how many bowls of tiger chowder he'd had and wouldn't he care for more, and before he
knew it they even got him to laughing when they started
reciting the very words he had used to praise its delicious
qualities before he knew what it was he was praising. And
most important of all, who had cooked what he was
praising.

Catfish finally wiped the tears out of his eyes long
enough to say that since Jib had done such a fine job he

should be assigned to help Sorry in the galley all the time.

That possibility sobered Shandy in a hurry.

"Catfish, you wouldn't really do that, would you? I mean, we need Jib to catch sharks; he's too good a fisherman to keep in the galley. He—"

The captain stroked the side of his nose and furrowed his brow thoughtfully. "Well now, I don't know . . ." he said to no one in particular. "I hate to lose a good cook and I hate to lose a good fisherman." He paused dramatically, then looked up. "I reckon the only fair way to do it," he shrugged, "is to wait and see which we need more, eh?" There was a twinkle in his eye.

Shandy heaved a sigh of relief. "Whew! Thanks, Captain," he murmured gratefully. "I don't know if I could take some of the surprises Jib knows how to cook up."

Now it was Jib's turn to grin like a porpoise. He was already telling Sorry about his Uncle Thigpen's recipe for gopher gumbo.

That afternoon Catfish changed his mind about leaving the wreck and heading for the deepwater curve. Fishing picked up in grand style and by sundown they had caught and Kip had tagged seven more big sharks. But none of them were tigers. Still, Sorry celebrated the day's good catch with a lavish supper of pan fried T-bone steaks. Unfortunately, by that time the boys couldn't have cared less. They were so tired they could hardly move.

"We'd best turn in early tonight," Catfish told the crew. "I want to be over DeSoto Canyon about daylight which means we'll pull out of here at three A.M." He looked at Rooster to make certain he understood.

"Okaydoky by me," nodded the chief engineer. "Who'll be upstairs?" Somehow the term "topside" had never found its way into the little Mexican's vocabulary. Sorry always claimed the term he did use was left over from Rooster's safecracking days. The crew had long since given up trying to correct him.

"I'll take the first turn," Catfish told them. "The rest of you be ready to turn out first thing in the morning."

Turn in or turn out, by now the captain's words held only snatches of meaning for Jib, who was slumped in his chair with his hands folded over his stomach. He looked as if he were contemplating where his T-bone steak had gone.

Shandy nudged him. "Jib, wake up. Time to go below."

"Ungh . . . huh?" Jib's eyes popped open and stared at Shandy.

"Were you asleep?" Shandy asked drowsily.

"Uh-uh."

"Then what were you doing with your eyes closed?"

Jib yawned. "Just looking at the backs of my eyelids," he answered matter-of-factly.

That night, Shandy and Jib slept as they had never slept before. They completely missed hearing the anchor chain clank in at 3 A.M. and were unaware that the trawler had gotten under way. The cool sea breeze that wafted through their compartment from the overhead deck hatch and the rolling lift and fall of the forecastle served only to lull them deeper into sleep. In fact, they were so comfortable in their cozy bulkhead berths that they overslept and missed their arrival at the 100-fathom curve by forty-five minutes. And then it was the different sound of the engine and a more subdued rolling of the trawler that finally broke the spell. With a shout, Shandy tumbled out of his berth and roused Jib. Quickly they dressed and scrambled up on deck. Catfish greeted them with a wave from the pilothouse.

The port gunwale of the *Elmira* was lined with dozens of trotline hooks, all connected to cables leading to a washtub full of coiled rope. Rooster, Big Clyde, and Sorry were baiting the hooks with chunks of bonito while Jonah tied one end of the rope to a fifty-five-gallon oil drum. Without asking what they could do, the boys got in line with the others and started baiting hooks.

"How far out are we?" Jib asked Sorry. "Are we over the DeSoto Canyon?"

"Seventy-five miles out and we passed the lip of the canyon a while ago at the curve," said Sorry. "From there at a hundred fathoms she drops off smartly to something like seventeen hundred fathoms."

"Goll-y!" gasped Jib. "What's that in feet?"

Sorry screwed up his mouth and didn't answer right away but he was calculating. All it took was a vacant look and a quick count of four of his fingers as they tapped his thumb and he had it.

"Ten thousand two hundred feet," he answered with authority.

"Gosh," said Shandy, "almost two miles of water under us."

"Ummm, yeah, I guess you could say that." Sorry went back to baiting again but Jib noticed he still stopped every once in a while to count something on his fingers.

Rooster ducked down into the engine room. Jonah called up to the wheelhouse. "Okay, Captain."

The *Elmira* moved forward slowly and Jonah pushed the oil drum off the stern. Rope began to whip out of the tub. Big Clyde started flipping over the baited hooks. Soon the rope was hissing faster. Big Clyde was flipping hooks with both hands, and Sorry and the boys who were baiting them had to work even faster. Just when it looked as if the hook flipping was going to catch up to the baiters, Jonah rolled another big oil drum over the gunwale, then tossed out a tall cane pole tied to blocks of cork to mark the spot like a big bobber.

The *Elmira* pulled off a half mile and another trotline went over the side. Two hours later, two more were dropped. After that Shandy and Jib were pretty well winded. Their arms were so tired they couldn't even get their hands to their faces to wipe off the fish scales. And by now the sun was well up in the cloudless blue sky and the day had all the earmarks of being a scorcher. Even what little breeze they had enjoyed earlier diminished until the surface of the sea was hardly rippled; yet the broad, slope-shouldered swells came and went with clock-like regularity.

Big Clyde strode over and squinted at the boys leaning against the deckhouse.

"You kids're okay," he said somewhat gruffly. "I figured at first ya just came along for the ride, but today I seen ya really working." He paused and sized them up with approval.

"We'd like to do our share," Shandy told him.

"Yeah, well you did fine with them yayhoos yesterday . . . better'n most landlubbers could do." The seaman jerked a thumb seaward. "Longlining 'em's a little different. You gotta be careful of them hooks. Saw a fella get pricked once when he was baitin'. Line flipped him over the side. By the time we got him hauled up he was drowned, hanging on that yayhoo line with the hook drove clean through his hand." Big Clyde shook his head and stalked off scratching his beard. Shandy and Jib sagged weakly to the deck.

The lumbering trawler wallowed through the gentle swells on a zigzag course while in the pilothouse Kip stayed close to his electronic gear in the hope that he might pick up the ping of another sensor shark. Sleek gray porpoises met and played around the trawler, then disappeared as quickly as they had come. Gradually the boys began seeing traces of seaweed on the water—brown, fibrous growth that appeared to be made up of tiny leaves and berries. At first it was scattered in small patches, then the patches grew larger until great masses of it covered the surface and stretched like an endless amber prairie ahead of them.

"Fishermen call it a grass line," Kip explained when Shandy and Jib asked him about it. "Tides and currents cause it. This one could have been built up by the compression characteristic of the Yucatan Current we've been following."

Catfish, who had been catching a couple of hours' sleep after Sorry relieved him at the wheel, slid out of his berth with a yawn and took a look at it.

"Wish we had time to work it for billfish," he said as he squinted at the growth. "Bound to be some big blues and sails around, thick as it is."

"Why?" asked Shandy. "Do marlin and sailfish like that stuff?"

"They sure do. They like what's under it—about a jillion baitfish hugging up under it for shade; that's what they want."

"Wherever you find anything floating on the surface like that you'll find fish," said Kip. "The tiniest ones come to hide while they feed . . . but the bigger ones aren't far behind them."

"Gee, there must be all kinds of fish under that weed," exclaimed Jib, "like people in a big apartment house."

Kip grinned. "From plankton you can hardly see in the attic, to marlin as big as a boat in the basement, Jib."

"And sharks," added Catfish.

Kip nodded gravely. "And always the sharks. Waiting in the sub-basement to pick off the stragglers. That, you can count on."

Catfish reached for the blower horn. "I hope that's what we can count on," he said. Then he called Rooster in the engine room and told him to cut down on the power. They were ready to put out the first longline.

Once again the baiting and hook throwing began but this time the boys thought it would never end. Before it was over, a mile of heavy line and hundreds of hooks went over the side to be buoyed and marked as had been the shorter trotlines that morning. It was just after this that Catfish noticed a ship on the horizon. He called to Big Clyde who was sloshing down the deck with bucketfuls of sea water.

"Take a look at her and see what she is." The captain handed a pair of binoculars down to the seaman.

The boys saw him study the distant ship through the glasses. Without hesitation the bushy-bearded ex-merchant mariner started growling out the details.

"Converted cargo transport, Cap'n, about three thousand tons. Eight winches. Cargo and trawl booms aft. Radar and plenty of electronic hardware in her rigging. Flying a Cariban flag and making about fifteen knots to the south-southeast." He handed the binoculars back to the captain.

"Thanks, Clyde." Pulling himself back into the pilot-house, Catfish glanced at Kip. "What do you reckon she's up to out here?"

"Hunting tuna, maybe. We're not far from the Gulf Stream and it runs right by Cariba's front door, you know." Kip paused thoughtfully. "Still, a ship that size carrying that much electronic gear is probably rigged for oceanography. In which case she could be up to anything."

They watched until the white speck disappeared over the horizon.

"No need to mention this to Rooster," Catfish advised the boys. "He gets real nervous when anyone mentions Cariba."

Visitors From the Depths

The next morning Shandy and Jib hurried to join the captain and Kip in the wheelhouse. But it was Big Clyde, poised in the bow, who spotted the action first.

"We got something, skipper!" he shouted.

One of the oil drums that tethered the line was weaving across the surface of the water. Abruptly it jerked under only to bounce up again and wobble off in another direction.

"Bring her three points off the starboard bow, Cap."

Catfish swung the trawler toward the bouncing drum. Rooster popped in and out of the engine compartment every few seconds.

"Steady . . . stead-eee . . ." Sorry leaned over the rail with a boat hook ready.

Rooster threw out the engine's clutch exactly at the right moment and the trawler drifted up to the drum. Sorry speared the rope and almost went overboard trying to hold it until the rest of the crew clawed it within their grasp.

Then there was a jumble of arms and legs as the men tugged, strained, and yelled all at the same time. "Get it up, don't let it slip!" "Watch out, he's a mean yayhoo!"

"Bet it's a lemon!" "Naw, it's a bull!" "Lookit what that sorry cuss did to the leader!" "Lower the boom!" "Somebody get a club—this yayhoo needs a headache!" "Hey, Kip! Where's your rifle?" "Here, gimme that gaff."

They ended up bunched in the stern, trying to drag the shark's broad head up out of water while its long brown body twisted and thrashed. Kip came on the run with his tagging gun. Jonah up-ended over the gunwale and slammed the long-handled gaff hook home. Rooster lowered the boom and a grappling tong went into the shark's gill slits. The engineer flipped a switch on the winch and the shark was reluctantly lifted part way out of water, snapping its massive jaws and twisting wildly on the end of the cable. Kip took aim and fired. The plastic dart impaled itself harmlessly in the shark's tough hide behind the dorsal fin.

"Shake it off," yelled Catfish, "there's another one a couple of hooks down."

The crew repeated the foray, this time bringing up a seven-foot hammerhead for tagging and releasing. In rapid succession, it was followed by two small blacktip sharks.

When the hooks were baited, the *Elmira* headed for the next trotline. Shandy and Jib, curious to know why Kip was tagging the sharks, scrambled down the companionway after him to the main cabin.

"Excuse us for bothering you," Shandy apologized. "But we were wondering if you could tell us something."

"Sure 'nough. Fire away," Kip said, opening a big black record book on his desk.

"Well, your tagging those sharks and all—is it because you plan on catching them again?" asked Shandy.

"No, I doubt if I will," Kip said, smiling, "but someday, somewhere, somebody might. You see, there's an address

and a number on each tag—a different number for each
fish. When somebody catches the shark we ask them to
mail us the tag and tell us where he was caught."

"Why have him do that when you already know where
he was caught?" frowned Jib.

"We know where he was caught today," said Kip, "but
maybe a month or a year from now that shark won't even
be in the Gulf of Mexico. Maybe he'll move into the
Atlantic and travel up to New York. That's what we're
interested in knowing—where he goes from here. His
migration habits. It's our way of learning a little bit more
about fish and how they live." Kip folded his arms and
leaned back in his chair. The corners of his eyes crinkled.
"Did you fellows know that some deep-sea turtles carry
radios with them so they can tell us where they're going?"

Both boys knew better than that. "Now you're kidding
us," said Jib.

"Nope, it's the truth," said Kip seriously. "Every year
there is a certain kind of sea turtle that travels hundreds
of miles to get to the Galapagos Islands to lay its eggs.
Now the Galapagos are a number of islands off the coast
of Ecuador in South America—no bigger than dots in the
Pacific Ocean. But the turtles always find them, no matter
how many miles they have to swim to do it. And the
strange thing is that they never get lost. Now how do they
do it?"

Jib scratched his head. "You got me," he said.

"I wouldn't even dare guess," said Shandy.

"That's exactly what we're trying to find out by giving
them radios—tiny transmitters attached to their shells
that send out signals so we can track them and study their
migration habits."

"Gosh, that's neat!" exclaimed Shandy. "Have you
learned anything yet?"

"Quite a bit," said Kip. "Enough to make some scientists believe that those turtles and others like them that travel tremendous distances to reach certain destinations are doing it by celestial navigation."

"By *what?*" asked Jib.

"By using the stars in the sky as a compass."

"Goll-y!"

"Do you think they *really* do that?" asked Shandy. "Are they that smart?"

Kip shrugged. "It's quite possible they are, Shandy. Right now it's only a theory. But one of these days we'll know for sure."

"What about sharks?" asked Jib. "Have those tags told you anything about them yet?"

"Our shark tagging program is still comparatively new," admitted Kip, "but we hope to learn a few things by tagging these sharks in the Yucatan Current. A few years ago when we tagged some sailfish out here we found that they went through the Florida Straits when the current system began to break down and followed the Gulf Stream up the Atlantic coast. There's no reason to believe the shark population in the Current will react any differently. But that's what we want to find out."

Rooster's curly head popped down through the hatch. "Trotline coming up," he yelled.

Kip and the boys hurried topside and the excitement of hauling in the lines and tagging sharks started all over again. Bull sharks, lemon sharks, thresher sharks, blacktips, hammerheads, and blues were taken and released again. But not one tiger shark showed up, nor did Kip's electronic equipment indicate there was one even near them in the area.

It was when they were rebaiting their last trotline that they had an accident. The trawler wallowed into a maverick wave and one of the branch lines fouled the propeller shaft.

Catfish signaled for power off and called Jib up to the pilothouse to stand by while he went down on deck to survey the trouble.

"Somebody's gonna have to go overboard and cut it free," said Big Clyde.

While the crew debated who was going to do it, Shandy took out his jackknife and pulled off his shirt and pants.

"I'll get it, Captain," he said eagerly.

Catfish paused an instant, then he nodded. "Put a line around him. Better give him your wire cutters too, Clyde."

With one end of a Manila rope around his waist and the other end held by the crew, Shandy climbed over the rail.

"Be careful," cautioned Catfish.

"Yes, sir." He slid down into the water.

For the next ten minutes he repeatedly dove to the propeller, sawed at the rope and clipped away at the leader cable, then sputtered to the surface to report his progress.

He had just ducked under again when Jib shouted, "Kip! Come quick—your radio—"

"Oh-oh!"

Kip sprinted for the pilothouse.

"Get that boy up!" ordered Catfish.

The crew hauled on the line. Shandy popped to the surface.

"What's wrong?" he asked.

"There's a tiger shark down there somewhere; come aboard!"

"But I've almost got it cut through, Captain."

"Don't argue. Get aboard!"

The crew reached down and started pulling him up the

side. Jib, who was leaning out of the pilothouse, glanced down into the clear blue water beside the trawler and saw something that made him catch his breath.

"Captain! *Look!*"

The crew scrambled to the gunwale and stared.

Coming up in a slow spiral from the depths beneath them was a shark longer than a lifeboat.

"Fry my hide, would you lookit the size of that yay-hoo!"

"It's a tiger all right. See those markings?"

Shandy shivered and hugged his shoulders. "G-gosh, what if it had come when I was under the boat!"

"You'd been in a sorry fix," muttered the cook grimly.

The giant tiger shark slid past the hull like a silent shadow and disappeared off their stern.

"Look! Look!" screeched the little Mexican. "He's after a bait!"

The farthest drum on the trotline was jerked abruptly underwater, then it shot out only to be jerked down again.

"What we gonna do now, Captain? That prop's still fouled."

"Rooster, get the winch hook over the side. We'll pick up the line and bring in the whole works—shark and all."

"Okaydoky, *Capitán.*" The engineer flew to the winch and started it up. The big boom lowered and Jonah stretched over the side with the cable and hook.

"Take her away!"

The cable tightened. As the grappling hook rose out of water the taut trotline came too.

"Swing it in!" shouted Catfish.

Jib hurried down from the pilothouse to join Shandy and lend a hand. Kip was right behind him.

"Everybody on the rope now! We gotta pull it forward

and tie it off so we can get another bite with the winch. Watch those hooks!"

Together the whole crew grabbed the shark line and strained. At the other end of the rope the shark went wild, smashing the sea with its huge body, furiously rolling and twisting with such force that water shot ten feet in the air.

"Lookit that devil fight!" "Get off my foot!" "Pull— we're gaining!" "Watch them yayhoo hooks!" "Back up willya?" "Who's tying it off back there?" "Hurry up, that's enough!" "Okaydoky, leggo!"

To a man they let go and the rope strummed from bow to stern like a giant guitar string. The shark hammered against its tautness with the violence of a battering ram.

"Pick it up, Rooster—he's all yours!"

The long arm of the boom reached down, Jonah slapped the winch hook under the line, and the little engineer started bringing in the biggest fish he had ever caught on the most unusual fishing gear the boys had ever seen.

In the excitement Kip disappeared for a minute. When he came back he was armed with Catfish's double-barreled shotgun. He opened its breech and jammed in two number 0 buckshot shells. As the winch hoisted the shark's head clear of the water, Kip leaned over the side and fired both barrels. Despite direct hits the tiger continued its thrashing rampage.

"Bring him up easy and get me a bat, this yayhoo ain't finished by a long sight."

Rooster complied. The monstrous head and snapping jaws appeared just over the gunwale. Its twisting, lashing tail section swung and smashed in the sea, showering the fishermen as they crouched back from the rail.

Big Clyde grabbed the baseball bat Sorry handed him and stepped up to the rail. Taking aim, he unleashed a swing that would have knocked a ball out of Yankee Stadium. The shark ceased thrashing.

"Okay, bring him aboard."

Deftly the boom lifted its big catch out of water and swung it over the side onto the deck.

"Nice work, Rooster. Shut her off."

Kip bent over the shark with his knife.

"Hey, Shandy. Now Jib can make you some more tiger chowder!" chortled Sorry.

Shandy grabbed his throat as if he'd been poisoned. "Arrrrgh!"

Jib didn't think it was the least bit funny.

It didn't take Kip long to open the shark and find what he was looking for. When he straightened up he was holding a round yellow sphere in his hands.

"Well, that makes two of them," said Catfish.

Kip nodded. "And this is the farthest out we've ever found one. I think we're on the right track." With his toe he nudged a coil of the trotline into a tighter circle and put the sensor in it to keep it from rolling. Then he glanced at Catfish.

"What would you think about heading south for a few miles and checking out the area with the radio until we got a signal? Then we could put out the trotlines and—"

"Hey, Cap'n, don't look now but I think we're fixin' to have visitors."

Everyone looked where Sorry was pointing.

Not a hundred yards off their port beam was the long, glistening black shape of a submarine.

To the Place of No Return

On the submarine's conning tower in large white numerals it said U-1059.

"I don't believe it! I don't believe it!"

Catfish turned to see what Big Clyde was mumbling about.

"What's wrong, Clyde? You never saw a—" The captain was startled by the sudden whiteness of the burly seaman's face. "Say, are you sick or something?"

"Captain . . ." said Big Clyde slowly, never taking his eyes off the submarine, "you can call me a blue-faced booby if you want . . . but that—that thing out there . . . it shoulda been dead and buried twenty-five years ago!"

"Good gosh," groaned Catfish, "he's slipped his moorings!"

"What do you mean, Clyde?" asked Kip.

"That sub—it's a three-gun German U-boat with a schnorkel. It don't belong here—it had to been sunk back in World War II!"

"Are you sure?"

"Sure I'm sure. I should know—I had five ships torpedoed out from under me by those things."

"Well, if you're right," said Catfish, "you'd better get ready to see some ghosts. They're putting over a couple of rubber rafts and it looks like they plan to come aboard." He nudged Kip. "Better call the Coast Guard and report it," he said quietly.

"Right." Kip headed for the pilothouse.

"They've got guns with them!" whispered Jib.

"Submariners always carry guns with them," Shandy told him casually. "It doesn't mean anything," he added hopefully.

Catfish strolled down the deck and pushed the Jacob's ladder over the side.

"Ahoy there!" he called to the closest of the two rafts. "Anything wrong?"

They didn't answer him but a man standing in the bow of the rubber raft was smiling. He wore light blue coveralls like the others, but unlike them he wore no black beret. He was bareheaded and had gray hair. He didn't speak or change his expression until he grasped the rope sides of the ladder, then he said:

"Permission to come aboard, Captain?"

"Sure," said Catfish. "C'mon aboard."

As soon as the man climbed over the side the rest of the crew quickly followed. Shandy didn't like the looks of any of them. They seemed nervous and kept their hands too close to the holstered guns at their sides. On their berets was a strange insignia: three bolts of crimson lightning in the shape of a K.

The leader, smiling, shook hands with Catfish and said his name was Captain Zarnoff. When he spoke his thin lips hardly moved, almost as if he were wearing a mask.

"Did you know your ship is operating in a restricted zone, Captain?"

Catfish bristled but he kept his voice even. "Not according to my charts, Captain."

"Ummm, yes," murmured the stocky submarine officer as he glanced around the deck of the *Elmira*. "This has been a militarily restricted zone for some time now." His eyes came to rest on the carcass of the tiger shark in the stern. "What exactly is your business here?" Without waiting for an answer he stepped around Catfish and walked toward the stern.

In three strides Catfish was in front of him, blocking his way aft. "Whatever our business is," he said slowly and firmly, his eyes never leaving those of Captain Zarnoff, "it's none of *your* business, Captain. Fact is, I reckon it's about time you explain—"

Kip shouldered his way through the armed group that had moved in behind their commander. He spoke politely but loudly enough for all to hear.

"Captain, this is a United States Naval vessel—what seems to be the trouble?"

Captain Zarnoff's eyes flicked over the tall, sandy-haired young man confronting him.

"The trouble," he replied coldly, "is that instrument you have there on your deck." Shandy saw he was pointing at the yellow sensor. "It is the property of the Cariban government. You are taking it illegally from these waters."

"I beg your pardon, Captain, but I believe if you'll look around you will see that this vessel has been engaged in fishing. And it should be quite obvious that the object you see on our deck came out of the stomach of that shark." Kip paused. "Naturally," he added, "in view of what you've told us, we'd be glad to give it to you—"

Captain Zarnoff glanced up.

"—providing, of course, you can prove it belongs to the Cariban government."

The submarine commander's face reddened. He snapped out an order in another language. One of his crewman jumped forward and picked up the sensor.

"Hey—!"

By then it was too late. The diversion was over. When the crew looked back, the men from the submarine were covering them with drawn guns. The sailors lost no time collecting the fishermen's knives. Zarnoff smiled triumphantly.

"I'll have to ask you and your men to come with us, Captain."

Catfish's jaw dropped. He thought he was hearing things.

Zarnoff's eyes shifted slowly down the line of fishermen. "You will only be questioned, nothing more. If you do as I say there won't be any trouble, and no one will get hurt."

"You're wrong, Captain."

Zarnoff glared at Catfish.

"I reckon you forgot about the penalty for piracy."

"That might not be a strong enough term for it," Kip spoke up quickly. "The military authorities I radioed two minutes before you boarded us, Captain, might be more inclined to call it an act of war." Kip emphasized the last three words, hoping their meaning would sink in.

If it did, the officer's face didn't show it. "Call it piracy or an act of war, whichever you wish," he said smoothly. "When your authorities arrive here I doubt if they will find evidence of either accusation." He looked around impatiently. "Now, all of you get into one of the life rafts."

The boys glanced at Catfish to see what he would do. They were amazed to see he was calmly lighting his pipe. He didn't look as if he planned to go anywhere. Jib snickered. Captain Zarnoff relieved one of the sailors of his automatic and leveled it at Catfish.

"Don't force me to make an example of you before your men," he threatened.

Catfish puffed away thoughtfully, befogging the air

between him and the sailors. Finally he said to his crew, "I reckon it's time we had a confab on the fantail."

Zarnoff frowned at the alien words. Then he understood. The fishermen were following the captain to the stern of the trawler. He would give them one minute to make up their minds, he said, then he would have to act.

The men gathered around Catfish. "What we do now?" asked Jonah.

"Not much we can do," said Catfish, his teeth clenching the stem of his pipe somewhat more forcefully than usual. "They got the drop on us—for now, anyway."

"I say we should rush 'em," Big Clyde doubled his sledgehammer fists. "Le'me get my hands on that runty little cap'n just once and—"

"Negative," rejected Kip. "It wouldn't solve anything. We're out here to find where those sensors come from, not to pick a fight. Maybe by playing along we can—"

"All right," called Captain Zarnoff. "You will have time to talk later."

The crew reluctantly went back to where they had been standing.

"Go to the side and get into the raft," ordered the submarine officer.

The *Elmira's* crew looked at Catfish. He nodded. "Okay, do as he says."

They responded as if they had intended to get into the raft from the very beginning—casually, without hurrying, stepping over the gunwale one by one and climbing down into the big rubber boat. Catfish was the last to leave.

"What about our ship?" he asked Captain Zarnoff.

"We will take care of it. Join your men."

There was a slight delay followed by the sound of running feet and shouted orders, then the men from the submarine clambered down the rope ladder and piled into

the second rubber raft. Quickly they paddled away from the *Elmira,* towing the fishermen behind.

"Sorry we can't help ya paddle," was Sorry's muttered contribution to their efforts.

"Whatdaya think's going to happen to us now, Cap'n?"

"I don't know," said Catfish, "but I got a hunch somebody put 'em on to us—somebody like that cargo transport we spotted yesterday. What do you think, Kip?"

"Could be. If she's the mother ship they may be taking us out to her. Then again, they may head for Cariba."

"*Cariba?*" The Mexican engineer shifted uneasily. He searched their faces. "You kiddin' Rooster, eh? Cariba— she too far off, no?"

"Not as far as you think," said Kip grimly.

The sleek submarine loomed big and ominous over them as they drew alongside. Six sailors armed with submachine guns waited on deck. Under their watchful eyes the *Elmira's* crew climbed aboard. The sailors motioned them toward the stern.

As they walked down the rounded deck of the sub toward an open hatch, Shandy glanced back at the *Elmira.*

"Captain! The trawler—!"

Everyone looked back at the gray vessel they had just left. The ship was listing heavily to port!

"Blasted varmints are scuttling her!" said Catfish. The crew stared in stunned disbelief.

"Golly—that's what Zarnoff meant when he said there wouldn't be any evidence around when the authorities came," Jib reflected. "We'll be gone and the ship will be sunk!"

"Dadblame it anyway," muttered Catfish. "First decent luck we've had in a couple days and we raise a sub and have our ship scuttled out from under us."

One of the submariners prodded him in the ribs with a machine gun.

"Okay—okay, we're going."

The crew of the *Elmira* climbed gloomily through the hatch and down the steel ladder leading into the dim interior of the U-boat. There another armed guard pushed them into a small compartment, then slammed a bulkhead hatch and screwed it closed.

They looked around. Several canvas and iron frame cots were folded and chained to the steel bulkheads on each side of them. Except for two small ventilators and a light overhead, the compartment was bare.

The boys lowered the bunks while the crew gathered around Catfish and Kip and talked over their predicament.

"The best way I can figure to handle it," said Catfish, "is to keep quiet about our real reason for being out here. As far as they know we're only shark fishing. That's all they need to know."

"What about us being in some kind of restricted area, Cap'n?"

"Hogwash," snorted Catfish. "Ask Kip."

"Certainly it is," said Kip. "We're not even near a

restricted zone—theirs or anybody else's—and they know it."

"Hey, we're moving!"

A slight vibration throbbed through the steel bulkheads, followed immediately by the muffled sound of water gurgling against the hull as they slid forward. After that there was nothing but a smooth, distant hum. The overhead light brightened. They were underwater.

Catfish pulled out his handkerchief and mopped his brow. "I reckon we might as well settle down in those bunks and get comfortable," he said. "They'll let us know when they want us."

The crew climbed onto the racks but they didn't feel much like resting.

"Hey, how about what them yayhoos did to the *Elmira*, huh?"

"Yeah, well, that runty admiral said he'd take care of it, didn't he?"

"That was the understatement of the day."

"He said all he wanted to do was question us, too," Sorry reminded them. "I hope he didn't mean with hot irons and needles under the fingernails—stuff like that."

Goosebumps raced down Jib's arms.

Big Clyde squinted up at the walls of their steel prison. "Say, Rooster," he asked under his breath, "you ever tried cracking a safe from the inside?"

"Shut up, Big Cheese!"

Three hours later they were aroused by the scraping of steel latches on the hatchway of their compartment. When it swung open a crewman came in with their dinners on tin trays. While he passed them out another sailor stood outside with a machine gun slung over his shoulder. Then they left and the hatch clanged closed.

"At least they don't intend starvin' us." Sorry prodded

his food cautiously. Then a terrifying thought occurred to the cook and his fork clattered to his tray. "You don't reckon they'd try to *poison* us, do ya?"

"Heck no. It's good food, eat it," said Catfish. "If they wanted to get rid of us they wouldn't do it this way."

Sorry's Adam's apple bounced uncertainly. "Y-yeah, you're probably right, skipper." Sorry picked up his fork again but he had lost his appetite. He put down his fork and watched the others to see what would happen to them.

Jonah wasted no time with his supper. It disappeared, much to Sorry's disgust, in about three big gulps, packed down with his allotted two biscuits.

When he finished he looked satisfied. "Gotta admit it's better'n most grub we get." He hiccuped.

Sorry bristled. "How would you know, cluck? Ya eat like a whale. Somebody could feed ya bedsprings and you'd be happy."

The Greek slapped his stomach and rolled back on his bunk laughing good-humoredly. "Don't you worry, little cook. The more Jonah eat, the more tougher he get. He save his friend Sorry from the bad men or his name not Jonah."

Jib stuck his head out from his bunk and looked down at the grinning seaman below him.

"Why do they call you Jonah?" he asked curiously.

The Greek thumped his chest with his fist. "They call me Jonah 'cause this one tough Greek—so tough even a shark can't eat him."

"What do you mean by that?" asked Shandy.

Jonah's smile broadened. "When I was a boy not much older than you kids I went with my papa and my brothers in our boat for sponges out of Tarpon Springs. We divers. Hard hat divers, you understand?" He knocked his fist against his head to indicate he wore a diving helmet. The boys nodded.

"Well," he continued, "one day my brother and me down on bottom under Twelve Mile Reef cutting fine big wool sponges when this granddaddy shark come by and look me over. Right away I jerk head and hit knock valve to let off stream of bubbles. We do this to scare off big shark and barracudas. But this ol' granddaddy shark he too big and too smart to be scared of bubbles. He just swing around, open mouth big as a steam shovel and scoop me up."

"Gosh!"

"This Greek thought he sure done for. Big shark start swimming off with lifeline and air hose coming out corner of mouth. Then all a sudden he stop and shake all over. He find he swallow tougher Greek than he figure on. So he spit him out. I shut off escape valve and shoot to surface like balloon. Almost get bends but got one plenty big story to tell. After that everybody call me Jonah."

Jib shivered. "What was it like in there, in his mouth, I mean?"

Jonah shrugged. "Black like coal mine cave-in. I think he knock me little silly 'cause this Greek got no time to get scared. Just wanted out in big hurry."

"I'll bet you did," Shandy said in awe.

There was a noise at the hatch. The guards came in and took away their empty trays. After they were gone, Catfish glanced at his watch and said:

"If it's questions this bunch wants, it looks like they don't plan getting around to them tonight. We might as well turn in and wait for them to make the next move."

It was late the next afternoon before anything happened to the crew of the *Elmira*. The hum of the submarine's motors changed pitch and once again they heard the gurgling swish of water against the hull as she blew her ballast tanks and surfaced. A half hour later the motors stopped and they heard the shout of muffled orders, the clanging of hatches, the sounds of feet pounding across the steel plates overhead.

Finally the hatch of their compartment swung open and two bearded soldiers in baggy uniforms motioned them out with their rifles.

The crew was quickly herded up on deck and across a gangplank onto a cement pier. The boys were surprised to see they were in a large, busy harbor with piers on both sides of them where freighters were being unloaded. Behind the ships they glimpsed palm trees and white buildings. Uniformed soldiers carrying rifles or machine guns were everywhere, watching or supervising whatever was going on. The guards prodded the group toward a waiting truck backed up on the pier. As they climbed into the back of it, clusters of soldiers gathered to watch, talking animatedly among themselves. The crew sat on long wooden benches along the sides of the truck. As soon as the two guards climbed aboard, the tail gate was closed with a bang and chained. The guards didn't bother to pull down the flaps of the brown tarpaulin covering the truck but sat at the ends of the benches with their rifles across their knees. They both wore black berets and their long hair fell thickly over their open collars, their faces dark and grim behind the heavy unkempt beards.

The truck rumbled off the pier, passed several dirty gray warehouses, was stopped once at a guarded gate, then swung left into a wide boulevard with rows of palm trees on both sides.

Catfish spoke to one of the guards. "Reckon you could tell us where we are?"

The man acted as if he had not heard a word.

Catfish nudged his engineer. "See if you can get anything out of him, Rooster."

The little Mexican fumbled in his shirt pocket and pulled out a crumpled pack of cigarettes. He offered them to the guards with a broad grin.

For a moment they hesitated, then one of them gingerly took the pack. He tossed his companion a cigarette and pocketed the rest. Then he pulled out a cigar and made a grand gesture of lighting it.

"*Por favor . . .*" began the Mexican and rattled off a short sentence in Spanish.

The guard puffed a blue ring of cigar smoke in his face and laughed uproariously. Rooster smiled and repeated the question.

The other guard spat out the answer. "Cariba!"

Kip nodded. "Well, we guessed right. It's the only place in the Caribbean that would dock a renegade sub."

"See if you can find out where they're taking us," prompted Catfish.

Rooster asked the question.

The guard took the cigar from his mouth and flicked the ashes over the tail gate. When he turned back to the Mexican his lean face was expressionless.

"*La Chunga!*" The words seemed to stick to the back of his tongue.

Rooster sagged in his seat and Shandy saw his face turn the color of wet straw.

"What did he say?" asked Catfish.

The little engineer spoke with difficulty, as if he had the breath knocked out of him.

"*Capitán* . . . he say the name of a place nobody ever comes back from. *La Chunga* prison!"

Prisoners of *La Chunga*

The crew didn't see it until the truck crossed a long causeway and passed through the outer gates. Then they understood why nobody escaped *La Chunga* prison. It was an ancient stone fortress. The walls of greenish streaked coquina rock were at least ten feet thick and rose steeply on either side of them to massive, pitted, blunt-toothed battlements and turrets. Great corroded iron rings hung from the sides of the vaulted arch through which they passed and the tall gates that closed behind them were made of foot-thick ship's timbers banded with iron and studded with the heads of iron spikes. There were armed sentries at the gates, armed sentries walking the battlements overhead; and protruding from each turret was the ugly muzzle of a heavy-caliber machine gun trained on the courtyard below.

Despite the afternoon heat a chill ran down Jib's back as they climbed out of the truck. "I never wished so much I was somewhere else as I do right now," he whispered nervously.

Shandy swallowed hard. "Me too!"

The guards spoke sharply and motioned toward a narrow vaulted stone archway opposite them. Big Clyde glared at the soldiers but he finally led the way.

"Looks like they're putting us away for good," he muttered in his beard. "Sure wish we'd jumped those submarine yayhoos when we had a chance."

"They must think we're pretty blamed dangerous, sticking us in a sorry looking joint like this," grumbled the cook.

Inside the narrow stone doorway, a spiral staircase led downward, the worn stone steps growing narrower as they descended until the smooth, damp stone walls finally brushed their shoulders toward the end.

At the bottom was a large room. At the far end two soldiers looked up from a table where they were playing cards. Behind them was a long rifle rack with a half-dozen rifles standing in it. The single bare bulb dangling from a wire over the table cast weird shadows on the walls as the soldiers stood up. One of them scooped a ring of keys off the rifle rack.

"Welcome to *La Chunga*," he said in English, grinning and rattling the keys. "This place might not got all the comforts you Yankees like but you get used to it, huh?" Shandy couldn't tell if it was the poor light or what, but despite the soldiers' dark beards, their faces and hands were as pale gray as the walls around them. Both guards wore crossed bandoliers of ammunition over their shoulders and their uniforms looked as if they had slept in them a week.

Selecting one of the keys, the guard unlocked half of a double iron door opposite the table. As it squealed open on its ancient hinges, the air in the room suddenly grew moist and warm with an oppressing odor that reminded Shandy of dead seaweed left too long under a pier.

"This way to your hotel suite," said the guard, leading the way into the corridor. The soldier who had brought them down the stairs followed some distance behind.

Both sides of the passageway were lined with wood-planked iron-banded doors. In place of door knobs they had iron rings. They were so old and scarred they looked more like discarded hatch covers. Slightly lower than head level, each door had a vertical inch-wide slot as long as a man's hand.

Their footsteps echoed hollowly as they walked down the stone passageway. Occasionally they passed under a dim bulb dangling from the ceiling, and as they approached one of these the guard stopped and pointed to a round iron grille in the middle of the flagstone floor.

"There are only two ways to leave *La Chunga, mis amigos.*" His teeth glowed yellow in the dim light. "You go out in a box or you go down here to feed our pet sharks." He kicked the iron bars with the toe of his boot. The boys saw the reflections of a black pool at the bottom of the shaft. "We feed our pets nothing but prisoners," he said. Then he led them to the end of the passageway and unlocked one of the cell doors. They filed through the narrow opening into a dank dungeon of a room.

After the cell door slammed behind them and the key clicked in the ancient lock they waited until their eyes grew accustomed to the dim light, then they looked around. It was a small room but the ceiling was higher than that of the passageway. Near the top of the wall facing them was a wedge-shaped opening with two rust-encrusted bars over it, the hole barely wide enough to let in a thin beam of light from the outside.

On a ledge near the door Sorry found a half-used candle. He quickly struck a match and lit it. In one corner were the remnants of a rotten straw mattress that had been torn apart, the straw strewn along the wall in small mildewed piles. On the other side of the cell was a corroded iron rack suspended from the wall by chains. It too had a straw mattress but most of the straw had come out through the rotten fabric cover and was trampled under foot in the accumulated filth of the centuries.

"Look at those pictures and names on the walls," said Jib. "There must be hundreds of them!"

Sorry held the candle higher so they could see the inscriptions more clearly in the flickering light.

"Can you make out what they say, Rooster?"

"*Sí Capitán.*" The little Mexican's voice was barely audible. "They say words like 'liberty, equality, freedom' —words like that. Then the prisoners write their names."

"What's this one say?" asked Shandy, pointing to a carefully lettered message scratched deeply into the coquina just over the cot. Beneath it was a picture of a gallows with a hangman's noose dangling from it, and below that was a large cross shaped like a sword or crucifix.

Rooster took the candle and held it close to the wall.

"It say, 'Rafael DeSilva Rae, Christian . . . born 1748. Prisoner *La Chunga* 1770 to 1779 . . . The last to go of his king's ship *Orinoco*.' Then there are the pictures." Rooster shook his head and glanced at some of the other inscriptions. "They are all alike, *Capitán*. Very sad. Men's last words before they be put to death. They leave names behind so they may be remembered." His voice trembled.

"If those yayhoos think I'm scratchin' my name up there with the rest of their creepy guests they got another think comin'," blustered Big Clyde.

"That's right," agreed Jonah, anxious to change the subject. "How long you think they keep us in this rat hole anyway, skipper?"

"Shouldn't be long 'fore somebody comes to get us. They didn't go to all the trouble of taking us prisoners just to dump us in here and forget about us."

"Boy, I wonder what the Coast Guard is thinking right now?" said Jib.

"You can be darned sure they've figured out what's happened," Kip told them in a reassuring voice. "Probably scouring the Gulf for that sub right this minute."

Although everyone knew there wasn't much chance of their finding the submarine as long as it remained in port, it was still a comforting thought.

Catfish glanced around their cell again. "I guess the only thing we can do right now is to make the best of it. Let's see if we can get this place a little more livable while there's still some daylight left."

While the men gathered some of the cleaner straw from the old mattress and spread it out along the driest side of the cell so they would have something to sleep on, Jib and Shandy took the candle and looked again at the names and pictures scrawled on the walls.

"Doesn't it give you the willies, Shandy? All those names of dead people and stuff . . . kinda like inside a tomb."

"*Inside* a tomb!" A prickly feeling ran down Shandy's neck. "Good gosh, Jib . . . we're not dead yet!"

"You know what I mean."

"Sure, I guess I do. I was a little scared at first too," Shandy admitted. "How about those dates? Some of them are more than two hundred years old!"

"Yeah . . . and look at that picture of a ship. I bet it was a Spanish galleon!"

Jib was pointing to a two-foot-square section of wall that had been blackened by candle smoke. Some prisoner had laboriously scratched every detail of the ship in the carbon black and in time the moisture on the walls had made the picture as permanent as if it had been painted there.

Jib climbed up on the iron rack to get a better look at it. Suddenly one of the hinges pulled loose from the wall and the rack dropped with a scraping clank, sending him sprawling.

Shandy helped him up, relieved to find that he wasn't hurt.

"Let's see if we can get it back the way it was," he said.

While he lifted one end of the rack, Jib shoved the rusty pins of the hinge back into the crack in the slab of stone.

"Is it going to hold?" Shandy strained under the weight of the heavy iron frame.

"I think it will . . . okay, let go." Shandy lowered the rack.

The hinge groaned and some of the powdery mortar between the blocks sifted to the floor, but it held.

Jib examined their repair job with a critical eye. It somehow lacked a look of permanence.

"On second thought," he said with a sigh, "let's just sleep on the floor."

The boys rejoined the others who were conversing in undertones in the corner. Catfish and Kip were trying to find out from Rooster everything he had ever known or heard about the prison in the hope that he might reveal something that would help them out of their predicament.

"Is it true what the guard said? Have you ever heard of anyone who escaped from this place?" asked Kip.

Rooster nodded gloomily. "I have heard they tried. Many times. But I know no one ever has," said the little engineer. "The guard spoke what all Caribans know to be true. *La Chunga* has no burying ground. When the revolution was over many, many prisoners were brought here.

Some say more than five hundred a month. But after that no one sees them again." Rooster shrugged. "They are gone."

"Whatdaya mean gone?" asked Catfish. "They must still be here."

Rooster shook his head. "No, *Capitán*—gone. *La Chunga* is one big prison but not big enough to hold so many men month after month."

"What happened to them?" Kip asked.

The yellow light of the candle made the whites of Rooster's eyes glisten. "They were executed at the wall . . . then they went to the sharks."

For a moment no one said anything, then Big Clyde asked, "How come you know so much about this place? I used to shrimp-fish these waters years ago and I never heard no such tale as that."

"Well, I have," said Rooster. "My mother, she was Mexican, but my father, he was one very patriotic Cariban. We live in Mexico when I am young because my father hate how bad is the Cariban dictator here. But when the war of liberation start he come quick back to Cariba with my oldest brother to help fight with his people for freedom. Later, after the revolution, when things go bad again and the new leader makes everything worse than before, my father is very heart-sick. He say my brother and him will go back to Mexico because what is happening is wrong. That's when they are made prisoners and called traitors and brought here . . . to *La Chunga*." Rooster glanced down at his hands. "That's how I know of this place," he said in a quiet voice. "It is where my father and brother died."

The silence of the cell was broken only by the sound of men breathing. Finally, when Catfish spoke, his voice sounded strange, as if he had something in his throat.

"Dadblame it, Rooster, you never told us nothing about—well, about them, I mean."

"No, *Capitán* . . . some things are not so good for telling about."

Big Clyde started to reach an awkward hand toward Rooster's shoulder, than changed his mind and nudged him with his elbow. "I'll tell you one thing," he said somewhat gruffly, "just let one of them yayhoos lay a finger on you or any of us and there's gonna be some slow marching and sad singing going on around here and it won't be for none of us."

An iron door clanged in the corridor. Heavy boots echoed in the passageway. Then a key rattled in their lock.

"Looks as if this is it," whispered Kip.

Colonel Kamo

The cell door opened and the guards motioned them out with their rifles.

Sorry glared at them. "Found out ya made a mistake sticking us down here, didn'tcha?"

"Quiet!" snapped one of the soldiers. "Line up and follow me."

He led them down the corridor, through the guard room and up the steps. The other guard brought up the rear.

As they crossed the cobblestone courtyard the sudden glare of daylight blinded them. The soldier turned in at a wide portal with two soldiers standing guard on each side, their rifle butts resting on the ground. A stone stairway led up and to the left.

At the top of the landing was an ornately carved door banded with strap iron and supported by massive hinges shaped like winged porpoises. On either side stood two guards in spotless green uniforms and black berets. Over their shoulders were slung submachine guns. Their belts and boots were highly polished. On the side of their berets was the same insignia the boys had seen worn by the men on the submarine—three bolts of crimson lightning in the shape of a letter K.

The soldier spoke to one of the guards. He looked them over, then turned and knocked on the door before swinging it open and stepping inside, closing it behind him.

A moment later he reappeared and held the door open for them to go in.

As the door closed behind them, Shandy was surprised to see that the guards had not come in with them. But that wasn't the reason he caught his breath and stared around him.

They were standing in one of the most luxurious rooms he had ever seen. A thick red carpet stretched out before them. The walls were paneled in mahogany and were hung with elaborately framed mirrors and oil paintings. And there were rich furnishings—a grand piano, over-stuffed chairs covered in red leather, cabinets and chests, statues, bookcases, maps—almost more than the eye could perceive.

"Come in, gentlemen."

At the far end of the room a man was seated behind a large desk. As they walked toward him, he stood up. He wore a simple brown uniform, no medals, no insignia. He was not much taller than Shandy but he was heavier and powerfully built. His head was shaved, his yellow-flecked eyes were pinched and drawn up at the corners and his right cheek was indented with a deep Y-shaped scar that drew one corner of his mouth upward in a perpetual smile. What bothered Jib was that the smile never got to the man's eyes.

"Sit down." He gestured toward a row of straight-backed chairs. "I am Colonel Kamo, Security Officer." His voice was low and harsh and he had a strange way of making each word sound like a question.

"Who is the captain of the trawler?"

"I am," said Catfish.

The officer sat down brusquely and glanced over some

papers on his desk. He closed the file with a snap and looked up.

"Captain, these are the charges against you." His face was immobile; the words clicked out tonelessly. "Your ship was operating in a restricted zone. It was equipped with electronic devices for spying. You were observed taking property belonging to the Cariban government. When apprehended you resisted arrest. When you attempted to escape, your ship was sunk."

"Somebody's been telling you fairy tales!" Catfish blurted out angrily.

"These offenses," Kamo continued, "render you and your crew liable to twenty years' imprisonment. Unless the prosecution chooses to press for the death sentence. In which case—"

Kip exploded. "You're crazy if you think you can get away with anything like that!"

Kamo flushed darkly but his voice remained calm. "Let me remind you that this is Cariba, not America. You have broken our laws and you will pay our penalty." Then abruptly his manner changed. He opened a silver canister on his desk and took out a cigar. "On the other hand," he continued, "if you will cooperate to the fullest extent with me, I can promise you your sentences will be less severe."

"Then maybe we get only ten years in prison, eh?" Rooster piped up defiantly.

Kamo acted as if he hadn't heard. He leveled his eyes at Catfish. "What was your reason for bringing your trawler into our waters?" he asked.

"We were shark fishing."

"I see." Kamo lit his cigar and blew a cloud of blue smoke toward the crew. "The electronic equipment aboard your ship—do you normally use this type of thing for fishing?"

"The trawler wasn't normally used for fishing," Kip

interrupted. "I'm a research oceanographer. The vessel was attached to our naval facilities in northwest Florida. Our work requires the use of this specialized equipment—that's why it was aboard."

Kamo smiled faintly. He jabbed the folder on his desk with his finger. "It says in this report that Captain Zarnoff found other rather unusual objects aboard—instruments that you claimed to have removed from sharks. Is this correct?"

Kip nodded. "We found them in the stomachs of tiger sharks."

"How many?"

"Two."

The Security Officer leaned forward. "How did you locate these sharks?"

Kip started to answer but changed his mind.

"Colonel, we're skirting the real issue here. Our trawler was boarded by a submarine crew based in Cariba. We were taken prisoners and our ship was sunk. Since we were in international waters this constitutes an act of piracy. So shouldn't you be questioning Captain Zarnoff instead of us?"

"I can assure you Zarnoff has been questioned. What I'm interested in learning is why an American vessel with a large amount of electronic equipment was operating in one of Cariba's restricted zones."

"I *told* you," insisted Kip, fighting to keep his voice calm. "If we were in a restricted zone we had no way of knowing it. Our charts showed that we were in international waters."

"And that's exactly where we were," added Catfish.

"Come, come, gentlemen." Colonel Kamo ground out his cigar in a ruby red ashtray. "This is a serious matter and we have no time to quibble." He took another cigar from the silver canister and tapped it lightly against the tips of his fingers, making the cellophane wrapper crackle like static electricity. When he spoke again there was a sign of irritation in his voice.

"The point is—you were discovered in Cariban waters taking property belonging to the Cariban government. I want to know who sent you, how you detected the spheres, and what your government knows about them."

"We've told you everything there is to tell," Kip answered truthfully. "We were shark-fishing and were unaware that we were anywhere other than in international waters, as our charts indicated. We found the spheres in the stomachs of tiger sharks we caught and assumed that they were something the sharks picked up and swallowed. We had no idea that they belonged to the Cariban government—in fact, we haven't the slightest idea what they're being used for. That's the whole story in a nutshell."

Colonel Kamo continued tapping his cigar. The corners of his mouth twitched. "You have a unique way of talking around a question," he said quietly. His eyes shifted to the others, the glittering yellow irises studying each face carefully. "Are each of you as adept at avoiding questions as your friend is?" The cigar rolled back and forth between his finger tips, the cellophane crackling loudly. "You—" His gaze settled on Rooster. "Would you like a month in *La Chunga's* dungeons to help refresh your memory?"

Rooster never flinched, nor did he reply. He simply glared back defiantly.

"Colonel, there isn't one of us who could tell you any more than we told you already," said Catfish. "Even if you were to keep us down in that rat hole of yours for a year."

"I see." The Security Officer looked at the boys. "That isn't an impossibility, you know." He seemed to be staring straight through them. The back of Shandy's neck began to tingle.

Colonel Kamo stood up and pressed a button on the top of his desk. "For the time being then, Captain, I suggest that you and your crew think it over while you enjoy the hospitality of my prison. Perhaps in a few days you will be more willing to tell me what I want to know."

The guards came in and stood behind them. The crew got up to go.

"The boys will remain here," said Colonel Kamo.

"Now wait a minute!" Catfish whirled around angrily. Without warning one of the guards swung upward with the butt of his machine gun. The blow caught Catfish on the back of his head. He grunted and slumped forward into Kip's arms almost before the rest of them knew what was happening.

"Captain—!"

Both guards jumped back and leveled their machine guns threateningly.

"You sorry bunch of—"

"Carry him and get out!" Kamo made an impatient movement with his hand and spoke sharply in Cariban to the guards. They prodded the grumbling men out of the room with Kip and Sorry supporting the unconscious Catfish between them. As the door closed, Kamo turned to the boys. A harsh laugh rattled in his throat.

"Now that the unpleasantness is over there's nothing to be afraid of, is there?"

Shandy shook his head slowly but Jib didn't move a muscle. He simply stared.

The corner of Kamo's mouth twitched with an innocent smile. "Tell me how the sharks were found," he asked softly.

Jib dropped his eyes.

Kamo looked at Shandy, repeating the question, the words louder and more menacing.

Shandy bit his lip, vainly trying to think of something to say—anything—to change the subject.

"Ah . . . Catfish—I mean, the Captain—used to be a commercial shark fisherman." He stopped, as if that were it. The answer.

"Yes, yes, go on," Kamo prodded impatiently.

"He . . . ah . . . we caught them on longlines—Japanese longlines. They've got lots of—"

An ominous shadow crossed Kamo's face. "Never mind that! How were the sharks with the sensors detected? What equipment was used?"

Shandy cleared his throat. He glanced at Jib but he was no help. Finally he decided it was no use. "I'm sorry," he said. "If our friends couldn't answer that, we can't."

Kamo's hand shot out. The blow caught Shandy on the side of his head, almost knocking him off his chair.

"Let me tell you something. We don't play children's games here. The only game we play is *my* game and it's called 'Life or Death.' Play it by *my* rules and you live; play it by any other rules and you die." Kamo straightened up. "For your friends' sake and for your own, I suggest that you tell me exactly what I want to know . . . otherwise your lives aren't worth *that!*" he snapped his fingers. The sharp, dry crack couldn't have been more meaningful to the boys if someone had fired a rifle in the room. "Now then, this electronic equipment—how did they use it?"

The boys clammed up.

In the foreboding silence the Security Officer took another cigar from his silver canister and lit it. Then, as if he had made up his mind about something, he tapped the cigar on the edge of his ashtray and turned to them once again. His voice was deceptively calm.

"Do you like shark fishing?"

"Yes sir."

"Aren't you afraid of sharks?"

Shandy screwed up his courage. "No, sir."

"And your friend here?" He looked at Jib.

"S-sharks and me always g-get along just fine," said Jib, following Shandy's lead.

"That's excellent," Kamo smiled, "because we have something in the cove outside the prison that will interest you." He pressed the button on his desk. "Perhaps after you've seen it"—the thin lips tightened over the yellowed teeth—"then we can have another friendly chat." He gestured toward the door as the guards came in. "Shall we go?"

Into the Shark Pen

As the colonel's jeep reached the end of the long, dusty limestone road, the boys saw on the other side of a tall link fence enclosure what appeared to be a small harbor or boat basin. Low buildings within the enclosure were ringed by guard towers and banks of floodlights. Between the road and the fence was a narrow canal that ended near the cove in what looked like a rectangular pool constructed of palm-stump pilings spaced at least a foot apart to let sea water flow in and out. A ship was berthed beside the pier and a cargo crane was drawn up near the pen. Soldiers with long prods were looking down at the water in the pen. And suddenly Shandy and Jib realized what they were looking at. The pen was alive with the thrashing, heaving shapes of huge tiger sharks!

"Get out," ordered Colonel Kamo. Their driver, one of the guards with the black berets, motioned with the muzzle of his submachine gun.

Kamo stopped them at the edge of the dock so they could see what was happening. Two soldiers near the crane heaved a large fish into the water. The pool's surface immediately churned with slashing fins. One of the men aimed a rifle at the sharks and fired. But instead of the usual explosion, the sound was more like that of Kip's tagging rifle.

Then the men with the prods moved forward, jabbing at the sharks and shouting. Finally they crowded around one end of the pool and it appeared they had singled out one shark to torment. Suddenly a gate in the side of the pen slid open; the shark was nudged into another enclosure and the gate closed.

Immediately the big crane rattled into action. Its steel cable lowered a sling into the small enclosure while the men jabbed with their prods. The cable drew taut and began to wind up. Before the boys' surprised eyes the big shark was lifted out of the pen, its long body supported by the sling, and strangely enough it offered no resistance. The crane turned on its tractor-treaded undercarriage and the shark was swung over the stern of the ship and guided down into what sounded like another tank of water on the vessel's fantail.

Jib nudged Shandy. "Was it dead?" he whispered out of the corner of his mouth.

"Uh-uh. Drugged, maybe. I think he used a hypodermic gun."

Colonel Kamo stepped forward and beckoned to a soldier in green fatigues who seemed to be in charge. The man saluted and talked with the Security Officer. Occasionally he glanced their way.

"Whatd'ya suppose they're up to?" whispered Jib.

"I don't know but I don't like the looks of it."

"Are you scared?"

Shandy glanced quickly at his friend. "Only half."

"Well, I am—all the way. My legs are wobbly."

"That's just from the boat. Don't worry, we'll be okay. If things get bad we'll fake a fainting spell or something."

Jib sniffed. "I doubt if I'll have to fake it. I feel like one coming on now."

Shandy frowned. "Well, hold it. We'll get out of this okay."

Jib wasn't convinced, but he did try to get his mind off his uneasiness. "I wonder what those long rods they're using on the sharks are?" he whispered.

"Might be some kind of electric cattle prods like—Shhh!"

Kamo had turned away from the soldier and was walking back toward them.

"What do you think of my pets?" he asked with unsmiling eyes.

Shandy avoided looking at the sharks. "Some pets," he murmured.

"Go over to the edge of the pen so you can see them better."

"Oh, we can see them fine from here," Shandy answered quickly.

"Get over there!"

The boys reluctantly edged closer to the black pool. They stopped a safe distance away from it, then Kamo's driver jabbed them in the ribs with the muzzle of his machine gun and persuaded them to go farther. In fact, he didn't let up until they were standing on the very brink of the pen. At that point, where they got a good view of what was swimming around in the water just below them, it would have been safe to say that Shandy was more than half scared, and Jib promptly lost any desire to faint.

The boys drew back as three huge sharks swung hungrily to the surface and rolled half over, their jaws gaping, their round, unblinking eyes fixed on them.

"What's wrong?" whispered Colonel Kamo behind them. "Do you find my pets disturbing? Don't be afraid. I

believe they've taken a liking to you." With a low laugh
he motioned to the Cariban he had talked to. The soldiers
had just goaded a drugged shark into the enclosure at the
end of the pool. Now they stopped and moved to one side
as if they were unsure of what was going to happen next.
The man in charge spoke sharply to two of them who
immediately put down their prods and began dragging a
long narrow plank out from beside the crane.

Keeping away from the edge of the shark pen, one of
the soldiers carried his end of the plank around the pool
to the other side, then they both walked it toward the
middle and laid it down. With both ends supported by the
dock the plank was hardly a foot over the water. The man
on the opposite side of the pen started to leave.

Kamo snapped an order angrily. The soldier stopped in
his tracks, his face ashen. The Security Officer uttered
three more words in a tone of voice that made chills run
down Shandy's spine. Whatever he had threatened, the
soldier obviously feared it worse than death. Hesitantly
he walked back and stepped up on the plank.

The simple act brought instant response from the
sharks. A half-dozen triangular black fins sliced up out of
the water as the dark shapes eagerly began patrolling
back and forth beneath the plank, the tips of their tall
dorsal fins almost touching it as they passed.

"Watch closely now," said Colonel Kamo in a hoarse
whisper, "because if you don't tell me what I want to
know . . . you're next."

Shandy looked around desperately for a way out of
their predicament but the Security Officer's hand closed
tightly on his arm, forcing him to watch.

Some of the soldiers called encouragement to their
luckless friend as he tentatively tested the six-inch-wide
plank. The boys couldn't understand what they said, but

they understood why the man hesitated. The shark pen was about twenty feet wide. Even if the man kept his balance the plank would probably sag under his weight until it touched the water.

Watching where he put his feet, the soldier took three uncertain steps forward. The plank sagged. The man threw out his arms to balance himself. His tense features glistened in the low, amber sunlight. He took another step. The sharks began roiling the water in the pen, working themselves into a frenzy of anticipation. With two more jerky steps the man was closer to the center of the pen. The water lapped over the plank in front of him. The sight seemed to hypnotize him. He stared at the wet spot, his face contorted. Kamo's hands tightened on the boys' arms.

"If he stays there they are sure to knock him off!" warned the Security Officer.

The soldier took another hesitant step and slipped, almost losing his balance. There was a sharp intake of breaths on the part of the watchers. He was sideways now, weaving back and forth. The plank swayed dangerously.

"*Madre de Dios!*" someone whispered.

Surprisingly, the man regained control and slowly turned himself in the right direction again. But just as he did, a shark rolled bottom-side up, opened its jaws wide and raked its rows of spiked teeth across the bottom of the plank with sufficient force to start the helpless soldier reeling again. With a sharp cry he lunged forward, staggering the rest of the way across the rapidly flexing plank, barely making it across as another shark rammed into the side of the pen, splashing water high over the dock.

Kamo relaxed his grip on the boys. The corner of his

mouth twitched nervously. From the expression on his face, he was obviously disappointed that the man had made it. His eyes bored into them. "Well . . . ?"

Shandy gritted his teeth. Jib tried to swallow but he couldn't. Neither of them uttered a word.

"All right. Then you're next!" Kamo shoved Shandy toward the plank.

As the guard prodded him the rest of the way he glanced back at Jib and knew that his friend was every bit as scared as he was. And that thought alone made him so mad that he was determined that he wouldn't show it. He wouldn't give them the satisfaction of seeing it even if—if Kamo had a million sharks in his pen! But then he stepped up on the plank and suddenly he was tingling like needles and pins all over. He tried not to think about what was in the water in front of him or what would happen if he fell in.

Clenching his teeth, he stepped forward. The soldiers crowded closer to the pen, murmuring. Shandy took another step and tried to calm his breathing. He told himself that walking the plank wasn't nearly as hard as walking a railroad track and he had done that lots of times.

Again his feet moved and this time the voices behind him hushed. The sharks rose to the surface and began milling around, their black fins cleaving the black water.

Shandy took a deep breath. He knew how much the plank would sag with a grown man, and if there was one other thing he had learned from watching the soldier it was that he couldn't stop. He would have to keep moving.

Summoning every ounce of courage he had, he started across, using his arms for balance, forcing himself to focus only on the rough board in front of him, forgetting the rest. Step after step, smoothly . . . with the plank sagging lower and lower. He heard a rush of water behind

him but he didn't stop. The plank suddenly arched upward and he almost lost his balance as a shark slammed
into it almost under his feet. He heard the rasp of sandpaper hide as another shape slid by, but now he was
moving fast, leaning forward and almost running. . . .
Just three more steps—two—one! Gasping, he leaped for
the dock and made it. He had made it!

Instantly the soldiers were at his side, grinning, laughing. Several patted him on the back and said words
Shandy knew were meant as congratulations. But all he
could do was grin back at them and nod his head. What
he really wanted to do was shout encouragement to Jib,
telling him not to think about the sharks, to keep moving,
to offer him some kind of assurance. But when he looked
across the pool he saw it was too late. Kamo and the
guard were already pushing Jib onto the plank.

The misgivings Shandy had had before were nothing
compared to those he had now as he saw Jib's face. Jib had
never been good at walking railroad tracks or keeping his
balance on anything that he couldn't hang on to. Even if it
meant slipping off a log and getting dunked in a creek, he
refused to get down on all fours and "coon" it. He got wet
instead. And it was with this same look of determination
that Jib started bravely across the plank, head up, eyes
down, concentrating on what he was doing the same way
he had seen Shandy do it.

The water in the pen began to heave and churn as fins
rippled toward the plank. Shandy clenched his fists and
clamped his jaws tightly together but his mind was shouting at Jib.

*Great! That's it . . . keep coming, Jib . . . you're do-
ing fine . . . you're okay . . . don't look away!*

He made it halfway without stopping. Shandy wanted
to whoop with joy. Jib was going to make it! When he was

three-quarters of the way, Shandy leaned out over the edge, reaching for him. And then it happened.

A huge shark rose halfway out of the water and struck the plank a glancing blow. Jib froze in his tracks.

"Don't stop! Keep moving!"

"I—I—"

Another shark grabbed the plank in its massive jaws and shook it like a bulldog. Jib lost his balance and started to fall. Even as he did, Shandy saw him glance toward the side of the pen and realize he couldn't make it. Instead, his feet slammed hard against the flexing plank and he made a wild, awkward dive for the end of the pen.

Only when he hit water did Shandy realize what he had done. Rather than fall into the main pen where he would have been instantly torn to bits, Jib had jumped for and made it into the loading enclosure with the one tiger shark everyone had forgotten.

Shandy was racing for the enclosure when two of the soldiers grabbed him and held him back. They shook their heads and shouted at him.

Shandy struggled free of them just as Jib bobbed to the surface. He wasn't looking at the dock, he was facing the half-drugged tiger shark that swam in slow circles around him.

Shandy snatched up one of the soldiers' cattle prods, yelled, "Jib!" and threw it.

Jib turned, his arm shot out and he caught it. Almost in the same motion he thrust downward just as the shark attacked, jabbing the tiger squarely in the middle of its broad head.

The shark veered away, lashing out with its powerful tail and smashing Jib sideways. The boy immediately took advantage of the situation by swimming hard for the side of the enclosure where Shandy and the soldiers hauled him out. He barely had time to wink at Shandy before he keeled over in one of the most realistic faints Shandy had ever seen.

Colonel Kamo pushed aside the soldiers and scowled down at him. "What's wrong with him?" he snapped.

"I—I think you *killed* him!"

The Security Officer's face turned a decided purple. He was so mad he even forgot to speak Cariban when he shrieked at the guard, "Take these two back to the prison and lock them up! I've had enough of this foolishness!"

The Plot

"By golly," growled Catfish in the flickering candlelight of their cell, "if I'd been there I'd have wrung his scrawny neck for putting you boys through all that!"

The rest of the crew expressed similar sentiments.

Shandy heaved a sigh of relief. "Thanks to Jib's fainting spell it turned out okay anyway. You should have seen how fast he snapped out of it as soon as the guard got us out of there. Boy, was Kamo mad!"

"That must have been pretty good acting," said Kip. "It sure was fast thinking, Jib."

Jib shrugged off the praise. "I didn't have to act very hard," he said in a somber voice. "It just came sort of natural."

As low-spirited as they were, the boy's unabashed reply brought smiles to their faces.

"Skipper, what you think they do with all them sharks penned up out there?"

Catfish glumly rubbed the lump on the back of his head. "Beats me, Jonah. From the looks of it everybody on the island is as nutty as pecan pie." The captain quickly glanced apologetically at Jib but it was too late. From the droop of his mouth the pecan pie thought had already gotten to him.

"Whatever they're up to with those sharks and sensors," said Kip, "Kamo acts as if it's some kind of state secret. I'm surprised he even let the boys—"

"*Listen!*" exclaimed Shandy.

"Huh?" said Catfish.

"That scratching sound . . . There it is again! Hear it?"

"Coming from over near the bunk," said Big Clyde as he snatched up the candle and cautiously advanced toward the darkened wall. The flickering yellow light and black shadows danced eerily over the rough coquina blocks with their ancient inscriptions.

Big Clyde got down on his hands and knees and searched under the iron rack. Nothing moved in the piles of dirt and decayed straw.

"Sounds louder from over here," said Kip, leaning over the end of the rack.

Big Clyde crawled around and put his ear to the wall. A look of distaste twisted his features. "*Rats!*" he snarled. "Trying to burrow in!" He doubled his fist and smashed it against the block with all his might twice.

The scratching stopped. Suddenly there were two answering thuds.

"By thunder, if those are rats they know Morse code!" said Catfish. "Stand clear and let me down there. Somebody's trying to get through from the other side!"

He dropped to his knees and rapped the wall with his knuckle three times. It was immediately answered with three raps. Then the scratching commenced again.

"Who's got something to dig with?"

Everyone felt through his pockets.

Finally the cook said, "We're cleaned out, skipper.

Those sorry sub sailors swiped our knives on the trawler."

"Well, there's one thing they didn't get." Catfish fumbled at his waist and came up with his big brass *Gott Mit Uns* belt buckle. Clutching it firmly, he began hacking at the wall as if it were a block of ice. Bits and pieces of coquina shell flew in every direction. In the excitement, Shandy leaned too heavily on the old iron rack and once again its ancient hinge pulled loose and sent the frame crashing to the floor in a cloud of dust. Catfish almost jumped out of his skin. Then he bounced back to the wall with a startled exclamation.

"Hey! When that thing fell this whole block moved! Let me see that candle a minute."

Big Clyde held it close. In the dim light they saw a wide crack where the hinge had been. It didn't go all the way through, but the mortar around the entire slab of coquina had been loosened. Catfish attacked the weakened joint with a vengeance. In short order the *Gott Mit Uns* buckle widened the crack appreciably.

"I think I can push it through now." He glanced up at the others. "Clyde, cover the door in case the guard comes. The rest of you stand back and give me some room."

Shandy held the candle while Catfish sat down and braced his feet against the block.

"Y'all set?"

"Go ahead, skipper."

Catfish pushed.

For a moment nothing happened. Then slowly the block began to give. With one slurring grind it slid through the wall, leaving a hole just large enough for a man's shoulders.

Suddenly an excited voice spoke to them from beyond the black opening.

"Do you speak English?" whispered Catfish.

"Yes, yes!" came the hoarse reply. "I'm sorry we have no light. We're out of candles."

Shandy handed Catfish the candle and he pushed it through the opening. Two dirty, disheveled faces blinked and peered owlishly back at them. One man had white stringy hair and an unkempt beard; the other was dark-skinned with curly black hair and the features of a Cariban.

"We heard them bring you in," said the bearded man eagerly. "We tried to attract your attention before but you didn't hear us. I'm Doctor Karl Hoffmann and this is Miguel Vargas, my friend. You are Americans, aren't you? What are you doing here?"

Catfish quickly explained what had happened, how the trawler had been sunk and they had been imprisoned for no apparent reason.

Dr. Hoffmann seemed relieved. "Thank God it's only that. I thought maybe . . . You see, we've been prisoners for two months with no word from the outside world."

"Well, you haven't missed much," said Catfish. "Things been going on just like always. What're they holding you for?"

Dr. Hoffmann moved his hand as if he were brushing a spider web from his face. He stared at Catfish and for an instant a look of suspicion clouded his eyes.

"Y-you *are* Americans, aren't you?"

The captain assured him that they most certainly were.

"I'm sorry . . . for a moment I—" He leaned forward, his voice a low, urgent whisper. "We must escape this place at once! Your country is in grave danger!"

"What do you mean? What kind of danger?"

"There is to be a war. A terrible war!"

Catfish frowned. He glanced at the other prisoner. The man nodded solemnly.

"Doctor Hoffmann is a nuclear scientist," he said quietly. "They've tortured his body but his mind is clear. He speaks the truth, *señor.*"

Catfish turned his head and called Kip.

"I heard," said Kip. "Tell him to go ahead."

Dr. Hoffmann crawled closer to the opening. His face was haggard and drawn. He paused to collect his thoughts. When he spoke his voice faltered at first but grew stronger as he continued.

"I am an East German—a nuclear physicist, as Miguel said. Because of my background I was invited to work for the Soviet Union, to continue my research in Moscow. I was developing a miniaturized nuclear device capable of producing an extremely powerful thermonuclear reaction —a radio-controlled explosive to be used in the manganese mines at Transcaucasia. Special transistorized components were being made for the device in China."

"You mean Red China?" asked Kip.

"Yes. I was in Peiping on a business trip when China and the Soviet Union broke off negotiations. Instead of deporting me back to Russia, the Red Chinese sent me here, to Cariba, where I was told I could complete my work away from the distractions of the outside world. Since Cariba was on friendly terms with both China and Russia, I wasn't unduly alarmed. It was only when I learned who Colonel Kamo was and what he intended to do with my invention that I realized what was really happening."

"He told us he was the Security Officer."

Dr. Hoffmann shook his head. "He's much more than that. He owes no allegiance to any country but his own. He's head of KLTCH, Red China's Central Intelligence System. The worst part is that he plans to use my nuclear device to instigate a full-scale nuclear war between Russia and the United States—a devastating war that neither side could win, leaving Red China in a position to dominate the world."

"He must be out of his mind," said Catfish.

"He's a fanatic, but an extremely clever one."

"He'd have to be a magician to pull off a trick like that," Kip remarked skeptically. "How could he do it?"

"I am the magician, and I'm afraid I've given him the means to do it," said Dr. Hoffmann.

"How?"

"By penetrating your marine defense system with radio-controlled sharks carrying nuclear bombs capable of destroying entire ports and coastal missile-launching centers such as Cape Kennedy."

"That's impossible," said Kip. "Our sonar stations would detect the things long before they were within range."

"Would they?" asked Dr. Hoffmann. "Remember, your sonarmen are trained to listen for the sounds of ships or submarines and to disregard the sounds of fish."

"But we rigged electronic equipment aboard the trawler to home in on the sensors. That's how we located those we found."

Dr. Hoffmann smiled faintly. "That was excellent," he said. "I dare say Colonel Kamo would be intrigued by that."

"But why wouldn't he know that it's possible?" asked Kip.

"He's a soldier, not a scientist," said Dr. Hoffmann. "I purposely led him to believe that the bombs would be completely undetectable—and unfortunately, for all practical purposes they are. The spheres you found were simply tracking devices; the nuclear components are to be added later, once Kamo is assured that the sharks can be directed to their coastal targets. I should imagine that your trawler was able to detect the sharks only at extremely short range; am I correct?"

Kip nodded. "I'm afraid so, Doctor."

"Then only when America has the equipment to scan hundreds of miles underwater to detect the ultra-low-frequency spheres, and the means of detonating them far at sea, is your country safe. That's why I say it is imperative that we escape *La Chunga*, that I get to America at once before it is too late."

Catfish looked up sharply. "You mean there's something that can be done?"

"Yes, I know an effective countermeasure," said Dr. Hoffmann quietly. "A way to jam the low-frequency controlling band and reverse the process so that the spheres can be detonated before they reach their target areas."

"That's the only reason they have allowed him to live," said the Cariban. "Kamo knows there is a countermeasure but he must learn what it is or China will never have absolute control over the weapon."

"How do you figure in this?" asked Kip.

"He was arrested with me," explained Dr. Hoffmann. "I was trying to give him information about the plot in the hopes that his underground group could get it to America. Unfortunately, Kamo's secret police got to us first. They believe he's only a messenger for the underground and can be made to divulge vital contacts. If they had known who he really was," whispered the doctor, "they'd have executed him on the spot."

"This I promise you," said Miguel Vargas, "if you can help us escape, I can have you and the doctor on your way to America in a matter of hours."

There was no doubt that the man meant what he said.

The only trouble was that neither Catfish nor Kip could see what they could do about it.

"As much as we'd like to help," said Catfish gloomily, "it looks like we're in just as bad a fix as—"

There was a noise in the corridor.

"The guard!" whispered Miguel.

Shandy blew out the candle as Big Clyde called a warning from the door.

"Quick! Push back the block!" Catfish told the Cariban.

The guard's boots thundered in the corridor.

"*Hurry*—"

The block of stone groaned and moved slowly.

Only One Way Out

They were on their feet just as the block slid into place and the cell door swung open.

Two guards came in. One of them carried a trayful of wooden bowls. The other stood just inside the door with his thumb hooked under his cartridge bandolier while he casually kept his rifle leveled at them. The man put down the tray and the guards left, slamming and locking the door behind them.

Catfish breathed a sigh of relief and everyone relaxed. He passed a bowl of soup and a wooden spoon to each of them. "Can't say as it looks like much but we better eat it to keep up our strength."

Sorry slouched against the wall, drawing up his knees and supporting his back with his shoulders so he could balance his bowl in the hollow of his stomach. For a long moment he contemplated its contents with obvious suspicion. After several cautious sniffs he finally dipped in his spoon, gave the concoction a stir, and dove in. The others awaited their cook's appraisal. It came quickly in the form of a choke, but since he had talked himself out of a perfectly safe meal on the submarine and was by now deeply regretting it, his only grumbled comment was,

"Like I always say, there ain't nothing like a steaming bowl of dishwater with a fish head floating around in it to make a man appreciate the finer things in life."

Jib and Shandy took a second look at their supper. Jib's eyes said no, his appetite said yes, but his Adam's apple decided the matter. Without a word he pushed his bowl aside and concentrated on satisfying his hunger pangs with dreams of finer things—his mother's homemade pecan pie with peaches and whipped-cream topping for instance. Shandy finally mustered enough courage to swallow some of the soup's broth, but it went down hard. His main worry at the moment was whether or not he could keep it down.

"What did you find out from the men in the other cell?" asked Big Clyde. "From over by the door, I couldn't catch much of what you was whisperin' about."

Catfish repeated what the German scientist and the Cariban had told them.

"They didn't have any suggestions about how we might get out of this place, did they?"

Catfish shook his head. "We never had time to get to that but I reckon if they knew a way they'd been long gone before now."

The crew ate their soup quietly.

"If what the doctor says is true," said Kip, "you can be sure Kamo won't be letting us go."

"Then this Greek says we better find a way on our own."

"There's seven of us and only two of them," said Big Clyde. "We could jump the guards and make a run for it."

Catfish vetoed the idea. "That might get us out of the dungeon but not past that gang topside. We wouldn't have a prayer. Somebody'd get shot for sure."

Rooster reminded them of what the guard had said, that the only way out was in a box or in the belly of a shark. "I don't think I much like neither way," he added with emphasis.

It was stifling hot in the cell and the men pressed themselves against the damp wall, trying to absorb some of its coolness. While the men were talking, Shandy kept thinking about the hole in the floor of the passageway with the grille over it. The guard had said it was where prisoners were thrown to the sharks. Unless it was a pen of some kind, those sharks came from the sea. And if the shaft led to the sea, then there was a way out of the fort. It took him a while to do it, but he finally persuaded himself that if the Caribans were catching and penning up tiger sharks so they could feed them sensors, then maybe there wouldn't be so many sharks hanging around that shaft as the guard said. And if that were the case, why then . . .

He got up and walked over to the cell door. It was made of iron and the ancient lock looked big and strong. The keyhole was at least two inches long and a half inch wide. Jib joined him.

"Got any ideas?" he asked quietly.

"Jib, what would you say it would take to open that door?"

His friend looked it over. "I'd say it would take a stick of dynamite."

"Yeah, I guess you're—" Shandy's eyes narrowed as he remembered something. He glanced at the flickering candle sitting in the middle of the floor. "Jib, I think maybe I do have an idea!"

They hurried back to the circle of light and with growing excitement Shandy outlined his plan to Catfish and the others.

When he finished, Catfish smacked his fist into the palm of his hand. "By golly, it just might work! What do you think, Kip?"

"It's a chance—if they don't hear us."

"You remember when we came down here we saw that the guard room was on the other side of that locked door at the end of the passageway?" said Shandy. "There wasn't any window in that door. They shouldn't hear."

"I ain't too hep on that disposal unit out there in the hall," said Sorry warily. "We might be jumping from the frying pan into the fire for all we know."

"What the boy says is right," spoke up Big Clyde. "If they been collectin' them yayhoos for some kind of experiments they ain't likely to be swimming around at the other end of that shaft."

"How do the rest of you feel about it?" asked Catfish.

"I'm with you, Captain," said Jonah. "I been swallowed once by a shark and lived."

"It's okaydoky by me, *Capitán*," said Rooster. "I don't think I like their jails already."

Catfish looked at Jib. "You're the one running the risk, lad. Do you think you can pull it off?"

"Yes, sir. I-I'll try."

"What about Doctor Hoffmann and that other man—Miguel?" asked Shandy.

"They'll go with us, of course." Catfish got to his feet. "We'd better give them the word. That guard might come back any minute now."

They slid the stone block back just far enough to talk to the men in the next cell through the narrow crack.

Dr. Hoffmann assured them that he was ready and willing to make any effort to escape. Miguel again promised that if they once got clear of the fort his friends could hide them where they would be safe.

Catfish told them to be ready, then he pushed the stone back in place.

They didn't have long to wait. They soon heard the door at the end of the passageway clang open, then the clatter of a key in the lock of the adjoining cell. Seconds later the door banged shut and the key rattled in their lock. Jib braced himself.

As the cell door swung open, the guard headed for the trayful of bowls. The soldier with the rifle stepped just inside the door, and at that instant Jib leaped forward and started beating him with his fists.

With a snarl the soldier flung out his arm and knocked the boy sprawling across the cell. He quickly swung his rifle toward the others, then the corners of his mouth slowly twitched into an ugly grin.

"*Qué hombre!* What a man this kid is! Not like the rest of you Yankee chickens."

With a guttural laugh he backed out of the cell while the man with the tray followed. The cell door slammed shut and the lock clicked.

Nobody spoke until the guard's heavy footsteps died in the passageway, followed by the final clang and thud of the last door.

Quickly they huddled around the candle. Jib held out his fists and opened them. In his left hand were two rifle cartridges and in his right there were three.

"Good boy!" whispered Catfish.

"Like a magician," praised Big Clyde. "I never even seen ya slip 'em outa his cartridge belt!"

"Good going, Jib!" said Shandy as Jib handed him the cartridges.

Shandy took out his handkerchief and tore a four-inch square of cloth from it. Then, wedging a bullet between his heel and the floor, he twisted and turned the cartridge until the pointed lead tip came loose. He did the same with the other cartridges and when he finished he poured all the gunpowder onto the square of cloth.

Then, picking up the candle, he broke it in two. He stepped on the bottom half until it was nothing but a pile of crushed wax and a three-inch length of wick. He laid the waxed string on the pile of gunpowder and twisted the cloth into a tight packet so two inches of the wick stuck out for a fuse.

"We'll know in a minute if this is going to work," he said.

Everyone crowded around the cell door. While Catfish held the burning candle, Shandy stuffed the packet of gunpowder into the key hole, leaving only the wick sticking out. Then he pushed the rest of his handkerchief into the slot with his little finger, packing it tightly.

"Where in the world did you learn how to do all this?" asked Catfish in amazement.

"From a movie," said Shandy. "It worked then and I sure hope it does now."

When the homemade bomb was all set, Catfish motioned everyone to stand back. Shandy took the candle and gingerly lit the wick, then stood back with the others.

Slowly the yellow flame crept up the waxed string. It seemed to burn forever. Then, as it disappeared into the black slot there was a blinding flash, a muffled explosion, and the lock had a hole blasted in it the size of a man's fist.

For a few seconds they choked and coughed from the acrid fumes. Then Catfish slid his hand through the narrow window slot and pulled. The door creaked open.

"It worked!"

"Quiet!—Listen!"

A hush fell over the cell. No sound could be heard in the narrow passageway.

While Shandy and Jib slid back the stone in the wall and helped Dr. Hoffmann and the Cariban through, Catfish and Big Clyde led the others to the iron grille in the passageway.

Hoping desperately, they tugged on it.

"Blamed thing's stuck," muttered Big Clyde.

"Lift, man! This is our only way out."

Each man grasped a bar and they all heaved together.

Gradually, with squeakings and scrapings that thundered in their ears, the heavy round grille loosened and came free. Carefully they carried it aside and set it down.

At the bottom of the dark stone shaft twenty feet below, an inky pool of water reflected slivers of yellow light from the single dim bulb in the passageway overhead. For a moment no one spoke. Shandy knew what was on their minds. He also knew what he had to do.

"I'm the lightest one here," he whispered. "I go first. If there's a way out I'll find it and swim back and tell you."

"Hold it," said Catfish. "This is a man's job. There may not be a way to get you up out of there if—"

"We haven't time to argue," said Shandy as he climbed into the hole.

"Wait—"

"Don't worry—I think I can work up or down easy against these rough sides."

Then they saw what he meant. He was bracing his body with his back and elbows on one side of the shaft while his bent knees and feet gripped the other. By slowly rocking himself back and forth, he worked his way down the shaft almost effortlessly.

But when the water was just beneath him and he glanced back up to see the circle of white faces peering down at him as if from a tiny round window, his throat tightened.

Forcing himself not to think about what might be waiting a few feet beneath him, Shandy let his body slip quietly into the still water. Its dark warmth crept up and engulfed him and the sharp taste of brine came to his lips.

He paused while his heart pounded furiously. Then he cautiously explored the shaft as far as he could reach with his feet. From what he felt, the shaft ended near his knees. Below that there was nothing.

Looking up again he tried to get his bearings, tried to remember where the cell was and which way the barred window to the outside had faced so he wouldn't swim in the wrong direction. When he thought he had it right he inhaled and exhaled as deeply as he could several times, then holding his last breath he pulled himself underwater.

As soon as he cleared the bottom of the shaft he swam slowly toward what he judged was the outer wall of the fortress, using a breast stroke and frog kick but getting his arms forward quickly in case he should run into an obstruction.

After several strokes he reached up, expecting to feel the rough stone of the prison. He touched nothing. Gradually he floated higher. Then almost before he realized it he popped out of water.

For one fearful second it was so dark he thought he had come up in some underground room. Then he gasped in relief. Sparkling overhead like tiny diamonds were stars. And a few feet behind him was the ominous vertical black shape of the fort's wall. He had actually swum some distance beyond it.

He looked in both directions. There was nothing to see, but he heard and felt the gradual rise and fall of the sea as it moved against the stone wall on either side of him.

Now, if he could just find his way back to the shaft again. He took a deep breath and ducked under, swimming back the way he had come. This time in the water ahead of him he saw the faint yellow glow of the lighted shaft. He had no difficulty slipping back into it and surfacing.

The eager faces still looked down on him and he quickly told them what he had found. Catfish whispered to the others, then Shandy saw Jib climb into the shaft and start his descent.

When his friend was directly above him, Shandy slipped underwater and waited as Jib did the same, then keeping close to each other, they swam out to the wall.

One by one the others crawled down the shaft and were helped the short distance to the surface by both boys. Catfish came last and as he wedged himself just inside the mouth of the shaft he quietly replaced the old grille over the opening. Minutes later he was with the others outside, clinging to the slime-slick outer wall of the prison.

"I know the way," whispered Miguel. "Stay close. I will lead you."

Following the Cariban they slowly pushed themselves along the base of the wall. It seemed to go on for miles. No one spoke. Once, someone's big hand reached back and pressed Shandy hard against the stone just as a powerful beam of light from above probed quickly at the black water in front of them, then swung away. A minute later they relaxed and moved again.

In the distance Shandy heard the low moan of a siren but he couldn't tell whether it came from inside the prison or from the pale glow to his right which he guessed was the harbor.

A short while later he heard another sound—waves hissing softly on a beach somewhere ahead of them. Then he touched bottom and looking up he realized the steep wall had become a long causeway and the prison was behind them.

Trying to keep from splashing, they staggered ashore and stumbled up a gradually sloping sand beach lined with slender palm trees. Beyond them were a few dim lights—street lights—and the shapes of buildings.

Stealthily the Cariban led them along the beach a short way, then turned in. The crunch of sand and broken shell underfoot was replaced by the quiet rustle of grass. Just as they entered the shadows of the palms, a figure leaped out in front of them.

"*Manos arriba!*" Light reflected off a rifle barrel.

"What'd he say?"

"He say 'hands up,' " whispered Rooster.

"Oh noooo. . . ." Sorry's groan trailed off into the night.

Enmeshed

Even before the cook's anguished cry died on his lips, Kip grabbed the soldier's rifle barrel with one hand while unleashing a powerful uppercut with the other. The surprised guard sprawled backward over a palm stump and hit the ground like a sack of meal.

"Wowee!" gasped Shandy.

Miguel picked up the fallen rifle and felt through the soldier's pockets, relieving him of a handful of cartridges and a box of matches. "This way," he said.

He led them to a wide boulevard and motioned for them to wait in the shadows. Across the street the buildings and stores were dark, their windows covered by steel shutters. Miguel started across, then stopped in the middle of the street. He was kneeling down, lifting something out of the pavement. Then he motioned for them to come ahead.

"Hurry!" he urged. "Down here."

It was the opening of a manhole. The boys climbed down the rusty iron ladder as fast as they could. The others followed, dropping into the foul blackness of the sewer one after another. Miguel was last and he slid the heavy iron cover back in place behind him.

"Gosh!" whispered Jib. "It's as dark as fifty midnights down here!"

Miguel's voice echoed hollowly as he warned everyone to stay close together but to follow him as quickly as possible. Then they set out.

Where they went and how they ever made it in the maze of endless tunnels, the boys would never know. But somehow Miguel kept the group from taking the wrong turn in the darkness and guided them as swiftly and surely as if he had always been accustomed to using the subterranean thoroughfare.

When they finally came to a halt at a fork in the musty brick tunnel, they felt as if they had been going around in circles for an hour. Miguel struck a match and they saw another iron ladder leading upward to a covered manhole. Not far from where they stood they could hear the gurgling rush of water through other tunnels, and somewhere in the distance the rumble of a passing truck . . . the clanging of a streetcar's wheels against steel rails.

"We're near the waterfront," Miguel told them. His match flickered out and he lit another. "Overhead is a narrow street. Opposite it is a ship chandler's shop called *Los Pescadores*. I'll go first to make sure the way is clear. When I signal, the rest of you follow, but at intervals. Is that clear?"

The men nodded.

Slinging the rifle over his shoulder, Miguel climbed the ladder. At the top he placed his ear against the cover and listened. Then he cautiously pushed it upward, slid it aside, and climbed out.

Seconds later, he beckoned from the doorway of the dark shop across the street and they climbed out, one after another, and made their way there. Catfish paused only long enough to replace the manhole cover.

As the door closed behind them they were led past shadowy counters to the rear of the shop. Someone pulled aside a large tarpaulin, there was a rapid exchange of voices speaking excitedly in Cariban, then a light was turned on.

"Miguel!"

For a split second a half-dozen men seated around a table stared back unbelievingly, then suddenly they swarmed across the room and engulfed the man they had given up for dead. They touched, they pulled, they laughed, they clapped Miguel on the back, and they all talked at once. In the midst of it all Miguel was returning their greetings with the same kind of enthusiasm while at the same time he was trying to introduce the others and begging everyone to speak in English for the benefit of

"*mis amigos* from the *Estados Unidos* who helped us escape." After that, the boys could understand most of what was being said.

"Man, we thought they had showed you the firing wall, Miguel!"

"Who, *him?* Not *El Primero*. Not even *La Chunga* can hold him!"

"Hey, *jefe*, how many of those rodents did you have to exterminate getting out of that rat trap?"

"Whoa, now," laughed Miguel. "Let me tell you about that." And without sparing a detail, he did.

Meanwhile Shandy and Jib took a closer look at their new surroundings. They were in a large storeroom stacked literally from floor to ceiling with oars, anchors, huge piles of nets, lanterns, brass ships' compasses, boxes of tools, barrels of rope, nails, and tar. Along the walls and ceiling hung large woven funnel-shaped baskets Shandy recognized as lobster traps. In the loft overhead the boys saw sails and loose piles of canvas rolled, stacked, or draped over the flimsy-looking platform reached by a wooden ladder leaning against one end.

"What kind of place did he say this was?" Jib asked Shandy in a low whisper.

"A ship chandler's shop. I think that means they sell things to fishermen and people who own boats—sails, oars, tackle, stuff like that." Shandy picked up a handful of brass screws from a keg and sifted them through his fingers.

"Boy, this place has got everything, all right," marveled Jib. "Sorta reminds me of my Uncle George's garage—no matter how long you look you never see it all. It's better even than going to a museum."

When Miguel finished talking the boys were suddenly aware that they were the center of attention.

"Shandy and Jib were the real engineers behind our escape from *La Chunga*," added the underground leader. "They are so brave, not even the sharks can scare them!"

With that, everyone broke into another laughing, back-slapping spasm of congratulations. When the furor finally slackened, all the ex-prisoners were made comfortable at the large round table under the sail loft where the men served them slabs of white goat cheese, wine, bread, and fruit. While they ate, the talk turned to more serious matters.

"The important thing now is getting you safely off the island," said Miguel. "There'll be no problem; we've done it many times before."

"How long before it can be arranged?" asked Kip.

"In about two hours. At midnight."

"Say, that's great!"

"Why will we be leaving at midnight?" inquired Dr. Hoffmann. "Won't our departure be more noticeable then?"

"Not at all, Doctor. That's when the Cariban night fishermen leave the port to set out their nets."

"I see; then we'll be disguised as fishermen?"

"No," said Miguel, "I'm afraid it won't be as simple as that. The harbor guards check the identification papers of all fishermen, going or coming. The one thing they don't check is the nets."

"You mean we're going out rolled up in one of those things?" Catfish jerked his thumb toward a pile of brown mesh net heaped in the corner.

"Like so many big fish," Miguel said with a grin.

"Then what?" asked Kip.

"The fishing boat will take you to a small cruiser we have moored in the harbor for just such emergencies.

You'll find it stocked with food and water. Other necessities are hidden beneath false floorboards in the boat. From that point you'll be on your own."

"How much chance we got of making it?" asked Sorry.

Miguel dropped his eyes and it was a moment before he answered. Finally he said, "With much luck and God's help you should make it all right. But I must warn you, government gunboats patrol the area constantly. They work overtime trying to prevent us from getting people out. The week before I was imprisoned they caught four boats of refugees and machine-gunned them all—men, women, and children. The gunboats are fast, well equipped, and heavily armed. You must be constantly on the alert for them."

"If we're able to give them the slip I guess we'll be in the clear, won't we?" asked Big Clyde.

Miguel shook his head. "You won't be in the clear at any time. As soon as Kamo learns that the doctor has escaped, he'll be tearing the island apart looking for him. You can be sure he won't forget to scour the sea either."

Rooster shivered. "You know, I don't think I like this escape plan too much already."

"I'm sorry I have to paint such a bleak picture about all this," Miguel said, "but I want you to understand what you're up against. We'll do everything we can to keep the odds on our side. As soon as you are on your way, our underground radio station will alert your Coast Guard with a coded message telling them you are coming and giving them your approximate position at sea by dawn tomorrow morning. One of their flying boats should pick you up without any trouble."

"Providing that *we* don't have any trouble," said Catfish.

"Exactly," said Miguel.

Kip glanced over at Dr. Hoffmann. "Doctor, this plot you told us about—how does Kamo plan to get Russia and the United States involved in a nuclear war simply by launching these swimming missiles of his from Cariba?"

"Sharks carrying the nuclear warheads will be launched at sea from Cariban tuna trawlers and oceanographic ships using powerful low-frequency guidance transmitters," explained Dr. Hoffmann. "These sharks will be guided to their target areas in two main echelons, then broken up into splinter groups to concentrate on individual targets."

"Which targets?"

"Primarily the Key West submarine base and naval station, and Cape Kennedy. Others will be sent into major ports along—"

"How?" asked Shandy suddenly, breaking in with a question that had bothered him for a long time. "How do they steer sharks like that?"

Dr. Hoffmann smiled and tried to explain the process in words the boys would understand. "They are guided by an extremely small electronic device, tinier than a transistor, that has been inserted in their brain. When this device receives a certain radio signal, a millimicrovolt of electricity stimulates either the right or left side of the shark's olfactory lobes."

"What're aw—awfactry lobes?" asked Jib.

Kip came to Dr. Hoffmann's assistance. "Jib, a shark's brain looks like a lopsided hourglass—the upper half is larger than the lower. We say a shark has a 'brain of smell' because the biggest part of it—this upper half—contains two sections that tell him exactly what he smells. So we call these his olfactory, or sense of smell, lobes. They are connected to sensitive olfactory tissues in the shark's right and left nostrils. And you remember I told you that if the scent of food a shark picked up was stronger in one nostril than the other, he turned in that direction? Well, I believe that's the way Doctor Hoffmann means the sharks are guided by remote control."

"Precisely," said the scientist. "The device in his brain stimulates him to turn right or left; the tracking signal transmitted by his sensor enables those on the ship to triangulate his exact position."

Jib nodded. "It sounds complicated," he admitted, "but I think I understand it now."

"What happens when the sharks reach their targets?" asked Kip.

"On radio command they will be detonated."

Kip frowned. "But with the sharks underwater, the explosions couldn't do much damage, could they?"

"Let's say there would be sufficient damage to suit Kamo's purpose. Harbor installations will be demolished. The submarine base at Key West would be crippled. Coastal gantries and missile launching sites at Cape Kennedy would be destroyed or contaminated. Any ships within the immediate area would be blown to radioactive dust and those within a mile of a single explosion would have hulls so laden with radioactivity it would have to be sandblasted off before they would be safe to use."

Kip whistled under his breath. "That sounds bad enough."

"Yes, but not quite damaging enough, as you pointed out," said Dr. Hoffmann, "and this is the important part."

"I don't get you."

Dr. Hoffmann leaned forward, his voice low but loud enough for all to hear. "Immediately following the explosions, Captain Zarnoff will beam a message in Russian from his submarine at sea. It will tell your military authorities that Russia has penetrated U. S. defenses with a secret nuclear weapon and unless America capitulates immediately, it will be destroyed."

"That's absurd!" exclaimed Kip. "Just because we have a couple of bases knocked out doesn't mean we'd give up the ship altogether."

"No, by golly!" said Catfish. "We'd fight back with everything we had—even throw the kitchen sink at 'em if that was all that was left."

Dr. Hoffmann nodded slowly. "That's exactly what Colonel Kamo hopes you would do."

"Huh?"

"Of *course*," answered Kip. "Retaliate in kind. Start the big one with Russia so that Red China can scrape up what's left. Oh, brother . . ."

"Tell me this," asked Big Clyde, "that sub out there—it's not Russian; it's German. An old U-boat. What's it doing here? And that guy, Zarnoff—how come he's working for Kamo?"

"You're right about the submarine," said Dr. Hoffmann. "The Russians captured it during World War II and sold it along with other military equipment to Red China. Kamo has convinced Zarnoff that if he cooperates now, he will be given command of the ex-Russian navy once Red China comes to power."

"In other words," growled Big Clyde, "the yayhoo sold out his country and turned traitor."

Dr. Hoffmann nodded.

While they had been talking, several of the Caribans had spread out one of the long brown nets that were stacked in the corner. Suddenly there was a distinct odor of fish in the room.

Miguel got up from the table. "It's almost time," he said

quietly. "The truck will be here soon for the net." He solemnly shook hands with each of them.

"Aren't you coming with us?" asked Shandy.

"No." Miguel smiled at him. "I wish I could but we have a great deal of work to do here before Cariba is again free. Perhaps one day, eh?" He gave Shandy's hand an extra squeeze. "*Vaya con Dios.*"

Then, one by one, the crew and Dr. Hoffmann lay down on the net while the Caribans wrapped and wound it snugly around their bodies.

"Phew-ee!" gasped Jib. "It smells like fish! I won't be able to eat another one as long as I live!"

Shandy was too busy holding his breath to offer a comment. The last he saw of Jib he was holding his nose with both hands. Then the brown, fibrous net closed tightly over them.

The Valley of Death

At eleven-thirty a truck rumbled up to the front door of the ship chandler's shop and three men climbed out. They unchained the truck's tail gate and went inside the shop. A few minutes later they and a half dozen other men came out of the door slowly with a long, bulky rolled net hoisted on their shoulders. Between each man the thick net looped down almost to the cobblestone pavement like the massive brown coils of a monstrous python.

With utmost care the great net was lifted into the rear of the truck. The men climbed in with it and slammed shut the tail gate. The driver got in, started the motor, and the truck rumbled off down the street toward the waterfront.

From inside the net, Shandy got some idea of how a trapped fish must feel when the tight meshes ensnare it. He was bound so tightly he couldn't move, and wasn't too certain he was still breathing. He felt hot, cramped, blinded, smothered, and squeezed all at the same time. The only thing he seemed to be able to do all right was to hear. Even then, the sounds were muffled.

Suddenly the truck jerked to a halt. There were questioning voices, a pause, then the truck started again. A short distance later it stopped, the cab door slammed, the truck bed vibrated and the tail gate banged against the rear bumper. The big net with its human cargo was slowly slid out. Once again Shandy felt the strange sensation of being trussed up in a bundle, hoisted to a man's shoulder, and carried away feet first.

Next, he knew the net was in a boat because he felt the bottom shift slightly as the boat listed. Then came the sound of an engine being cranked, the cough of an inboard starting, the boat scraping a piling as it moved away from a pier.

Somewhere in the distance a ship's whistle boomed its deep voice across the harbor. A bell rang. Then everything was silent except for the soft whisper of water against the hull.

What seemed like forever to Shandy passed in a matter of minutes but finally the inboard sputtered to a stop and eager hands were pulling at the net, loosening it.

The first thing the boys did was gasp for air, then help untangle the rest of themselves from the net. Silhouetted in the darkness beside them was a small cabin cruiser. Kip and Catfish climbed aboard and made a quick check of their supplies. There was plenty of canned food and five-gallon tins of water in the cabin's lockers, along with binoculars, charts, flashlights, flares, and even a sextant. Under the floorboards were the necessities Miguel had mentioned: several M-1 carbines and three Czechoslovakian 9-mm. folding-stock submachine guns with their cartons of ammunition. The fuel tanks were full and more were stored forward.

"We seem to have everything we'll need," said Kip.

"I reckon so," said Catfish. "Start her up, Clyde, and let's see how she sounds."

Big Clyde pressed the starter button and the engine roared into life. "She's hot as a firecracker, Cap'n."

"Good. Get the bow line, Jonah."

The Greek scrambled forward to untie the cruiser from her mooring buoy. The others leaned over the side and shook hands for the last time with their Cariban friends.

"Give our regards to Miami!" smiled one of the men.

"Sí, and take care for the gunboats," cautioned another as he shoved a handful of cigars into Rooster's hand. "The *Pilar* is a strong vessel. She will get you there."

Then they all waved and pushed their boat away from the cruiser. "Good luck!" they called.

Big Clyde slipped the *Pilar* in gear and she eased out of the harbor toward the black Gulf Stream.

With the sea wall behind them, Catfish's spirits rose considerably. "Well," he said cheerfully, "there's nothing between us and home now except ninety miles of open water."

"And maybe a few Cariban gunboats," added Sorry, less cheerfully.

It was a half hour later that the fog began to roll in and the sea smoothed to an oil-slick calm.

"This's the first time I was ever glad to see fog," Big Clyde told Catfish as he watched the glowing dial of the cruiser's compass. "Once we're in it those gunboats'll near about have to run us down to find us."

"You're all set on your bearings then?"

"Yessir. She's headed straight for Miami, Cap'n."

"Good. If we run into trouble, get into the thickest fog bank you can find. Kip and I loaded the rifles and machine guns. They're laid out on the bunks below in case we need them. I wouldn't mention them any more than you have to in front of the boys if I were you. No need to alarm them if we don't have to."

"Right, skipper."

The little cruiser churned along on her course with a slight porpoising roll while the crew made themselves comfortable in the cockpit. Catfish need not have worried about alarming the boys unnecessarily. Rooster was already filling them in with bits of information that left no doubt in their minds that they were in for an exciting night.

"They say all this water from here to Florida got one plenty bad name," he confided to them. "Caribans call it 'El Corredor de la Muerte' . . . how you say, 'The Valley of Death.'" He seemed pleased with his translation. "Plenty sharks and plenty killer boats—maybe more than one hundred! But don't you worry, we make it okaydoky." The little Mexican lit one of his long thin black cigars and puffed out a cloud of smoke that smelled to the boys like burning tar.

Shandy and Jib weren't really worried. The odds against their getting this far without being caught had been so great that they didn't seem to count any more.

At first the sky was clear and studded with stars but these were gradually snuffed out by the thickening fog. Now all they could see of the island were clusters and strings of red, yellow, and green lights, their haloed light shining palely along the waterfront.

It was Jib who noticed a red light climbing above the others in the sky. He pointed it out to Shandy.

Shandy studied it awhile. "It's moving awfully slowly," he said. "Maybe it's a helicopter or something."

"If it is, you don't suppose they'll be able to spot us out here, do you?"

"Not as dark as it is," Shandy reasoned. "Anyway it's probably just some airplane flying over the city."

For a moment the lights of the city blacked out, which

seemed strange to the boys, but then the red light also dissolved behind a swirl of gray mist. Several minutes passed before they saw the glow again; this time it was much larger and higher in the sky. Just as Shandy called Catfish's attention to it, a bright searchlight suddenly speared the darkness behind them.

"It's a gunboat! Look out!"

Big Clyde switched off the engine.

Now they heard the even throb of the other craft's diesels as it approached on an oblique angle to their stern, still too far away for the slowly swinging spotlight to pick them up.

The boys knew now what the red light had been—the port light of the gunboat. It had appeared to be going up in the air because it was coming toward them off their port quarter. Had the gunboat been approaching from the opposite direction, its green starboard light would have been the most visible.

The *Pilar* lay perfectly still while the clouds of fog drifted over, around and past it. Behind them in the still gray darkness the gunboat kept coming, its long probing white finger of light reaching ahead, first on one side, then the other, hunting something of substance in the flat gray nothingness.

Shandy held his breath when he saw how close it was coming to them. A rhythmic throbbing of engines filled the night and in the space of three heavy heartbeats it sounded as if the gunboat were going to ram them. But the long, gaunt shape slid past without seeing them, the searchlight still feeling ahead as the waves bobbled the cruiser and the sound slowly receded into the fog.

Shandy was surprised to find himself wringing wet with sweat. Everyone breathed a sigh of relief. No one talked or even whispered until the sound of the gunboat's engines had faded completely. Even then they waited another nervous ten minutes before starting up the cruiser's engines again.

Kip and Catfish brought the weapons up on deck. The boys were delighted when they were given two lightweight M-1 carbines like the other crewmen. Big Clyde, Kip, and the captain armed themselves with the submachine guns.

The boys noticed the cruiser wasn't moving nearly as fast as it had been. Big Clyde was feeling his way from one dense fog bank to another. They were hardly five minutes away from where they had stopped when Catfish suddenly shouted a warning. Looming out of the fog directly ahead of them was the waiting gunboat!

The *Pilar* heeled abruptly to port, engines racing. But not quickly enough to avoid the sudden flash and dazzling glare of the spotlight. Without warning the gunboat opened fire. Geysers of water spouted from the sea as the cruiser swerved to get out of the blinding light. Then everyone was firing at once until it sounded like a warehouse of exploding firecrackers, the *Pilar* fishtailing in and out of the fog with the gunboat holding tight to its wake.

"Get the light! Get the light!" somebody shouted over the stuttering bursts of machine guns and the popping crack of rifles. Lead thudded into the *Pilar's* wooden hull, shattering, splintering, ripping out whole sections of superstructure. The cruiser zigzagged violently, temporarily outmaneuvering the deadly four-foot geysers stitching the water behind its stern, the rapid *pow-pow-pow* of a heavy machine gun punctuating the crackle of smaller caliber fire that was rimming the gunboat with blue and yellow muzzle flashes.

With a splintering shatter the spotlight went out.

Big Clyde spun the wheel to starboard and the *Pilar* skidded into another fog bank.

Behind them sporadic gunfire continued to rake the night but the soldiers no longer saw what they were firing at. Then suddenly, before they could take advantage of the respite, the cruiser's engines abruptly sputtered and died.

Big Clyde hit the starter. It ground over and over but nothing happened. Catfish jumped to his side. "What's wrong?"

"She just gave up, skipper!"

Rooster was already sliding open the hatch to the engine compartment. His head and shoulders disappeared into the black hole. Even before he said anything they could smell what was wrong.

"*Ca-ramba!*" exclaimed the Mexican. He sat up, pulled off his shirt and began tearing it into strips.

"How bad?" asked Catfish.

"Bad as she can get, *Capitán*. Fuel in the bilge. Place leakin' like a sieve."

Kip ducked into the cabin to check on the damage, only to reappear minutes later with the startling report that the floorboards were awash.

Rooster lowered himself into the hold and began plugging holes with strips of his shirt. He worked fast but not fast enough.

"It's pourin' in faster than I can stop it," he called. "Better get me something for bailing, quick!"

The boys found two pails and a battered saucepan floating around in the bait well. In no time the crew had a bucket brigade going, Rooster filling them and passing them up to be emptied over the side. The bilge water reeked of gasoline.

"They hit our fuel tanks," said Catfish. "I don't need to

tell you to be careful," he cautioned them; "a spark would set us off like a Roman candle."

"Gosh," Jib panted, "we're a sitting duck for that gunboat."

"Sure," Catfish whispered huskily, "but have you ever tried to find a sitting duck that didn't want to be found? This fog is perfect cover . . . they'll have to stumble over us before they find us."

"What about their radar?" asked Shandy.

"If we're lucky we're close enough to be under it," whispered Kip. "A low-silhouette wooden boat is a poor radar target anyway."

Despite all their efforts the cruiser began listing heavily to starboard. Rooster popped out of the hatch, gasping for air. Shandy replaced him. Then Jib, Sorry, and the others took turns. After what seemed like hours of steady bailing their muscles ached with fatigue. But what was worse, they couldn't keep up with the steady flow of water through the bullet-riddled hull.

Catfish hated to admit defeat but there was nothing they could do. The *Pilar* was listing so badly now that just the weight of the men emptying buckets along her starboard side threatened to push the cockpit coaming under and flood the cockpit.

"Better let it be," he said finally. "Secure the hatch and everybody spread out along the port side. Maybe we can trap enough air below decks to at least stay afloat. How far you reckon we are from the Stream, Clyde?"

"Half mile, give or take some."

"If we can make it, it'll carry us toward home."

"What're our chances?" asked Kip.

"About fifty-fifty," said Catfish. "Currents are funny out here. They're just as liable to carry us in as out."

That brought a groan from Sorry. "I can just see us

drifting back into the harbor tomorrow morning. What kinda welcome you think they'd give us?"

"A warm one," promised Dr. Hoffmann, "you can be sure of that."

For the time being, at least it didn't look as if the cruiser was going to sink from under them. It tilted on a steep angle and stayed there while water sloshed and gurgled in the hold. Kip and the boys salvaged life preservers and whatever else they could from the cabin and dragged it up on deck along with a five-gallon can of drinking water they secured with a rope to a deck cleat. Several cans of orange juice and other goods were stuffed into a poncho and wedged under the roof of the cabin where it would be high and dry. After that there was nothing to do but hang on and wait for the night to pass.

Shortly after midnight they heard the sound of powerful engines. The boat had no lights and it was moving slowly through the fog somewhere off their port beam. It could have been someone who would have given them aid but they didn't dare call out. It might have been the gunboat. The sound of its passing and the lapping of waves against the *Pilar's* hull were all that betrayed its presence. Then even these died away to be replaced once again by the lonely silence of the mist-shrouded night. Clinging precariously to the tilting deck of their half-sunken boat, the uncomfortable crew finally drifted off into a fitful sleep.

Last Ordeal

Shandy awoke with a start. For a moment he didn't know where he was, then the grim gray shapes around him came into sharp focus and he knew the nightmare wasn't over yet. It was still going on.

Slowly he raised his head, wondering what had awakened him. His clothes were damp and he ached all over. Everything looked flat and colorless in the half light before dawn. But the fog had lifted and he was relieved to see they had drifted out to sea during the night. There was no island or boats or rescue plane in sight; nothing but the slate-gray sameness of the sea in all directions. He wished he could go back to sleep and when he awoke again it would all be gone and they would be lazing in the sun on the deck of Catfish's houseboat back at Phillips Inlet. But his lips were too parched, his throat too dry for sleep. He was terribly thirsty.

The five-gallon can of water was still tied to the cleat where Kip had put it the night before. Painfully, Shandy got to his knees. Taking care not to disturb the others he climbed over the sleeping figures and made his way up the slanting deck toward it.

Untying the rope, he lifted the heavy container up on

the gunwale and tilted it forward to unscrew the cap. Suddenly it slipped out of his hands, banged the cockpit coaming and clattered overboard.

Without thinking, Shandy lunged after it. He hit the water almost at the same time the can did, grabbing the handle just as it was sinking. Blowing and sputtering, he floundered to the surface while the shaky, wild-eyed crew lined the deck wondering what had happened to him.

"You okay?" Catfish called anxiously.

"Sure . . . fine." He felt a little foolish. "I was trying to get a drink and the can slipped out of my hands." He towed the container alongside.

"Good boy," said Catfish. "We couldn't afford to lose that." Big Clyde caught ahold of the handle and hauled the heavy can aboard. The others reached down for Shandy.

As he stretched for their hands something grazed his foot. Instinctively he pulled up his legs and kicked. His shins struck something solid and rough moving by under him.

Suddenly everyone was shouting at once, the water churned, and before Shandy's startled eyes a huge shark broke the surface, its hideous rust-colored body rolling like a log as it twisted back toward him, slicing the water with its tall, glistening fin.

Shandy's arms almost left their sockets as he was snatched upward, his shoulders and back raking the bullet-splintered planking when he was dragged over the gunwale into the cockpit.

No one heard his gasp of gratitude in the clamor of excited voices. "Man! You see how *close* that yayhoo came!" "Hey! There's blood on his leg!" "It's just a scratch, some hide off his shin. . . ." "Let him up, don't smother the kid!" "Yeah, he's okay." "Thank the Lord for that!"

Shandy sat up to show them he was really all right, just a little winded from the experience. "You fellas . . ." he forced a grin. "Boy . . . I was never so glad—"

"Easy, lad. Get your breath back first."

Shandy swallowed and nodded gratefully.

"From now on we better—"

There was a scraping rasp and something thudded hard against the hull.

"Hey!" exclaimed Shandy, remembering something. "*That* was the sound that woke me up!"

Big Clyde glanced over the side. "We got us some more visitors," he reported unhappily.

The crew looked to see what he was staring at. Instead of one dorsal fin they now saw five. Five long gray sharks were cruising in lazy circles around the boat, their lean shapes undulating grotesquely just beneath the surface.

"Give me one of those machine guns," whispered Big Clyde.

"Forget it," said Catfish, "unless you want every gunboat in earshot on our necks."

Big Clyde glared back at the sharks but he knew the captain was right. "Yeah . . . I guess it ain't worth the gamble," he said.

Clinging to the high side of the cockpit the crew kept a wary eye on their unwelcome guests. Without warning one of the sharks swung in toward the cruiser and struck the hull a thudding blow with its wide blunt head, rolling sideways as it slid by, scraping its rough hide against the planks. The sight sent a shudder of revulsion down the line of watchers. No one mistook the reason for the monster's action or the look in its cold, lidless round eye as it passed. The shark was sizing them up.

"At least we have guns if we need them," murmured Kip. And he wasn't thinking about gunboats.

The sun rose in a blinding white orb, casting a merciless glare across the sea. For an instant everything was dazzlingly bright, then color gradually seeped back into the world. From horizon to horizon the sky was a pale washed-out blue, but the water was a deep indigo with patches of bright green seaweed showing here and there. Tiny flecks of color swam beneath them, and deep down, floating on a level all their own, were dozens of lavender jellyfish drifting through the blue void like a gossamer fleet of flying saucers. Despite the presence of the sharks the sun's first warmth cheered the crew. But as the day lengthened and the sun bore down on them out of a cloudless sky like the heat from an open door of a blast furnace, their spirits began to wilt. By noon their depression was complete. With it came the painful realization of their plight. Home was more than eighty miles away. They had not been rescued because they were no longer what and where they should have been. They were nothing but a speck of wreckage drifting like any other flotsam on the rim of an endless sun-glazed sea.

Shortly after two-thirty in the afternoon as they were passing around the water can for each man's three-swallow ration, they spotted an airplane. It was a jet. At first they were afraid that it might be from Cariba but as soon as Kip looked at it with the binoculars he identified it as an American plane.

They leaped to their feet, yelling wildly, waving their shirts, the water can, anything they had at the hurtling silver speck low on the horizon. But the jet never altered course. Seconds later it disappeared from sight.

"He didn't even see us," moaned Sorry, dejectedly pulling his tattered T-shirt back over his blistered shoulders.

"Maybe he come back," suggested Jonah in a half-hearted attempt to raise their spirits.

"Yeah—and maybe they already give up looking for us too," said Rooster with a sigh.

"They won't give up," Kip assured them. "If the radio message was sent as Miguel promised, they'll keep looking until they find us."

"Providing we can last that long in this sun." Dr. Hoffmann tapped the water can and it echoed hollowly.

A strange look suddenly came over Shandy's face. "Hey—*listen!*"

Instantly they were on their feet, their eyes searching the sky.

"*There!* There it is!" Jib pointed excitedly at the airplane swinging in over the horizon, heading straight for them.

Kip quickly checked it with the binoculars. "It's an Albatross!" he yelled. "A Coast Guard Albatross!" With that they let out a whoop and waved everything they had.

"Did he say 'Albatross,' Captain? The same name as your houseboat?"

"That he did, Jib, but this one's a flying boat! And I can't think of a more fittin' namesake that I'd rather see right now neither!"

The sleek white twin-engine amphibian with orange and black markings droned in over them so close they could see the pilot's grinning face as he waved. Then the plane banked and came over them again. This time it dropped something small with a bright five-foot ribbon streamer trailing from it. The object plummeted into the sea ahead of the boat.

"What's that?"

"A marker to check wind and drift," answered Kip. "They're going to drop something else—probably a raft."

He was right. On the next pass the airplane roared in

not more than thirty feet over them and dropped a packet that was inflated by the time it hit the water practically at their bow. Big Clyde had it alongside as the plane banked and glided down for a smooth landing on the water.

While the big amphibian taxied closer, the crew climbed into the yellow rubber raft and pushed away from the half-sunken cruiser.

A large waist hatch on the side of the plane opened and a grinning Coast Guardsman yelled, "Hey! Any of you guys Americans?"

They bombarded him with yells.

"Well, what took you so long?" was his laughing reply. "You stop to go fishing?"

Friendly, eager hands helped them aboard and after that it was like a family reunion. Everyone was laughing, talking, kidding, and pounding everyone else on the back as if they hadn't seen each other for ages. Then the hatch was closed, the amphibian gunned its motors, swung into the wind and took off.

"How in the world did you fellas see us down there?" yelled Catfish over the droning whine of the engines.

"One of our jets spotted a reflection," said a Coast Guardsman. "He didn't want to chance tipping off any Cariban gunboats by taking a closer look, so he radioed us your position."

"I'll bet he saw our water can," said Shandy. "It's the only thing we had that was bright."

"Boy, this is one day I'm glad the sun was shining," Jib said fervently.

Kip looked over at the German scientist. "Well, Doctor, it looks as though we're going to make it after all. What do you suppose Colonel Kamo will do with his plot now?"

There was a twinkle in the doctor's eye. "Unless he is more stupid than I suppose, he will throw it in the wastebasket before it backfires."

Kip laughed. "I wouldn't be a bit surprised if that turns out to be exactly what he does."

Jib was gazing thoughtfully out the window at the sun-dappled sea. Suddenly his face lighted up. "Hey! I just happened to think of something!" he exclaimed.

"What's that?" asked Shandy.

"Those sharks of Colonel Kamo's. If he feeds them bombs now that we've got Doctor Hoffmann, he's sure going to have a bunch of sharks with a whale of a bellyache!"

"You're not kidding," Shandy agreed. "And you know something else, Jib?"

"What?"

"It couldn't happen to a nicer man."

ABOUT THE AUTHOR

ROBERT FORREST BURGESS names shark fishing as his favorite sport. A free-lance writer and photographer, he has ample opportunity for outdoor adventure, but he has always lived dangerously. As a boy he built diving gear to explore an old shipwreck sunk in 30 feet of water near Lake Michigan. In high school he took a job as a railroad section hand to get himself in shape for the better-paying job of climbing and painting high-tension wire towers. He volunteered for the Army Ski Troops at the end of World War II and spent a year in the Alps of northern Italy, and then returned in 1956 with his bride to tour Europe on a motor scooter. Mr. Burgess attended school through junior college in Grand Rapids, Michigan, continuing his college education at Michigan State University and the University of Neuchâtel in Switzerland. He has worked as a cartographer, and is a member of the International Oceanographic Foundation. His stories, articles, and photographs have appeared in many national magazines. He and his wife live in Chattahoochee, Florida.

ABOUT THE ILLUSTRATOR

Originally from Pennsylvania, Vic Donahue became a cartoonist for the Omaha *World-Herald* after one year at the University of Omaha, and won four yearly awards from the Artists and Art Directors Club in Omaha for his advertising designs. After two years as a feature artist with Newspaper Enterprise Association he became a free-lance artist, and since 1948 has illustrated many books for children. With his wife and two sons, he lives in Tucson, Arizona.